Would he take the lure . . . the *fatal* lure?

"Anything you wish," she said, turning her limpid brown eyes on him . . .

Inside the room he watched her shed her dress. His eyes glittered when her brown-nippled breasts came into view, bobbing as she discarded her lingerie. When she was naked, she came very close to him and asked huskily, "Would you like me to undress you?"

She removed his coat and his shirt, then unbuckled his pants and let them drop to his ankles. She reached into his shorts for his rigid member . . .

Her job was to keep his attention, and that's what she would use her considerable skills to do.

She had no desire to die.

ANGEL EYES

#4

CHINATOWN JUSTICE

Also by Robert J. Randisi

ANGEL EYES

#4

CHINATOWN JUSTICE

Robert J. Randisi

SPEAKING VOLUMES, LLC

NAPLES, FLORIDA

2012

ANGEL EYES

#4 CHINATOWN JUSTICE

ISBN 978-1-61232-586-6

To Anna and Christopher

CHAPTER ONE

THE CENTER OF San Francisco's lucrative and considerable gambling community was Portsmouth Square. Among the halls surrounding — and forming — the square were the Alhambra, El Dorado, Bella Union, Parker House, Dennison's Exchange, Frontline House and the exotically named Mazourka Arcade and Varsouvienne. They all offered essentially the same things: free food at the bars, music, pretty women — some for touching and some for gawking at — and gambling.

The music was supplied by musicians playing, among other instruments, violins and harps.

Since men outnumbered women in San Francisco by ten to one, many customers were happy just to be able to come in and exercise their "gawking" privileges.

More than anything else, the saloons offered gambling,

in all shapes and sizes. The most popular games were roulette, rondo, faro, poker and blackjack.

The only other sections of the city that offered rival at-
tractions to those in Portsmouth Square were parts of Sac-
ramento Street and all of the eastern side of Dupont Street.
These sections were in the city's infamous Chinatown,
where, among other types of gambling, dice and domi-
noes were also offered, and where a gambler sometimes
got the chance to risk more than just his money.

As Liz Archer rode through Portsmouth Square she
studied — with more than a touch of awe — the gambling
casinos and saloons that surrounded it. She had heard about
the Alhambra, the El Dorado and some of the others,
but this was the first opportunity she'd ever had to see
them, and she was impressed.

In mid-afternoon, however, the square was not as lively
as it became after dark, when hawkers, high-class prostitutes and one-man bands worked their magic on the crowds.
Wondering what the area would look like at nighttime,
Liz decided to change her original plans. She still had most
of the bonus she'd earned in the Dakotas hunting a wolf,
and there was no reason she had to find an inexpensive
place to stay while in town.

After all, what was money for if not to spend, and
enjoy spending?

Liz brought her horse, Blossom, to a stop in front of the
Alhambra. That was the hotel she had heard the most about.
She dismounted, took her rifle and saddlebags and entered
the fabled hotel.

The lobby alone was as large as most of the hotels she
had ever stayed in during her young life, and she made an

effort not to gape as she walked up to the huge front desk.

The clerk, a well-dressed young man in his late twenties, who affected — or attempted to affect — an aristocratic air, almost lost his composure when he looked up and saw Liz Archer standing there. Such was the effect her beauty had on men. She had learned how to handle it, and for now she ignored the clerk's reaction.

"Uh, y-yes. Can I help you?" the man asked.

"Yes, I'd like a room and directions to the nearest livery for my horse — "

"We can take care of your horse, ma'am," the man said, interrupting her. "We have our own accommodations for our guests' animals."

"Oh," she said. "Well, thank you."

He reversed the register—which was on the same oversized scale as the rest of the surroundings—and Liz wrote her name, and nothing more.

"That's fine, Miss Archer," he said. He struck a bell on the desk with his palm, and another man — this one younger, but no less impressed by Liz's beauty—appeared, wearing a red suit.

"Take the lady to room fourteen," the clerk said. He smiled at her and added, "I'll make sure your horse is cared for, Miss Archer."

The young bellhop made a move to take her saddlebags from her but she said, "I can handle it, thanks." Looking disappointed, he led the way to the large, ornate staircase that dominated the lobby. Liz followed.

She was gratified to see that her name was not familiar to the clerk — he had not recognized her as Angel Eyes. Not that she was ashamed of her reputation. She had decided, since leaving the Dakotas, that it was simply something she had to live with, like her arms, her legs, her *beauty* — all of which were things she was not ashamed of.

Why then should her reputation be any different?

It shouldn't be, she decided, and San Francisco was really the first town where she would try out her new outlook on life.

She followed the clerk to room fourteen, where he inserted the key and opened the door for her.

"Thank you," she said, handing him two bits and attempting not to look too overcome by the size of the room and its expensive, ornate furnishings.

She did not know if tipping was something that was done in San Francisco, and it never occurred to her that she might be giving the boy too little, but he grinned as if she had kissed him and said, "Thank you, ma'am. If you need anything — anything! — just call for me. My name's Thomas."

"All right, Thomas," she said. "I'll remember."

"Thomas," he said again, as if to impress it upon her indelibly.

"I'll remember," she promised.

He nodded happily, backed out of the room and closed the door behind him, leaving Liz to stare in frank admiration at her surroundings without feeling embarrassed about doing it with her mouth open.

The Chinese whore was lovely, with slanted brown eyes, a bee-stung mouth, a long black curtain of hair and proud, firm little breasts that pushed against her neck-high, red dress.

The man standing before her, however, had no interest

in her body at that moment. Though he admired the expanse of thigh that the slit in her dress revealed, he had other, more important things on his mind.

"You know who the man is?" he asked the whore.

"Yes."

"And you know what to do?"

"I am to make sure he chooses me."

"Will that be difficult?"

"If he likes Chinese girls as much as you say, it should not be a problem."

"It had better-not be," the man said.

He had been sitting on the bed in the girl's room and now he stood up. She smiled at him coyly and asked, "You would not like to stay with me for a while?"

"I came here to conduct business," the man said to her. "I do not need to get women from a whorehouse. Women come to me and ask me to take them. I wouldn't soil my hands with you, girl. Just make sure you do your job. Understand?"

"I understand," she said contritely. She knew that if she did not please this man he had the power to see to it that no man ever wanted her again. "I understand."

The man left the Chinatown bordello with a look of distaste on his face. He did not need to frequent places like this except for one reason.

He happened to own this one.

He walked to the end of Ross Alley and stopped to talk to the two men standing there in the deepening shadows.

"It's all set up. Make damned sure this is done right, Wilkes," he said to one of the men.

"Yes, sir," Wilkes said, and the man with him, whom

he had recruited for this job, nodded.

"I'll be at my home waiting for word that the job has been done."

"Yes, sir."

"If it hasn't," the man said, "I had better never see either of you again."

CHAPTER TWO

LIZ DECIDED to do some shopping while the shops were still open. She went to Market Street, looking for something dressy enough to wear to the casinos in Portsmouth Square, but not too dressy, because who knew when she'd have occasion to wear it again.

She settled on a suit that came with pants and a skirt, and she bought a new pair of boots to go with it. It was an expensive outfit, but she figured that if she was going to gamble she might as well spend as much as she could on herself before the casino took her money.

Thinking about gambling brought back memories of Chance Taker, the gambler she once thought she loved. She still had fond memories of him, but she no longer believed that she had truly been in love with him. Still, there was some pain involved in remembering how he had been shot and killed for cheating at cards, and how she had impetuously killed the man who had done it.

She was walking back to the hotel with her packages when she saw a man giving a young woman a hard way to go. From all appearances, the woman was a whore, but that didn't give the man a right to force himself on her if she didn't want him to.

Liz crossed the street to take a hand.

"Come on, lady," the man was saying. He was dressed in dusty trail clothes, a brawny man who was easily forcing himself on the woman, pushing her back toward an alley. "I just want a quick one in the alley, is all."

"Leave me alone," the woman shouted, but the man simply lifted her off her feet and carried her to the alley, while other men passing by saw and ignored the incident.

Liz followed them to the alley. She found them on the ground with the man on top of the woman. He had the bodice of her provocative dress ripped open and was pawing her naked breasts, trying to bring them to his mouth.

"That's enough," Liz said from behind them.

"Huh? What?" the man said, looking back. "Go away, girlie. Me and my friend want some privacy."

"No, we don't!" the girl cried from beneath him. "Please!"

"She's just a whore," the man said to Liz.

"Get up."

"Look here," the man said, getting to his feet and turning to face Liz. The woman sat up and tried to pull her dress closed to cover her firm breasts. "You shouldn't go butting into other people's business — "

"Move along."

"Lady," the man said. "I'm telling you — "

"And I'm telling you," Liz said. "Move on. The lady doesn't want your company."

"Lady," he said, laughing, "she's a whore — "

"And you're filth."

"Hey!" he said, poised as if to go for his gun. "If you wasn't a woman — "

" — you'd have backed down a long time ago," she finished for him. "You aren't man enough to stand up to a man."

"Look — "

"Now move along," she said, transferring her package to her left hand so that her right hand was free. He noticed her gun for the first time — and her apparent willingness to use it.

"You're all whores," he said in disgust. Easing past her, he left the alley. She turned and watched him until he was gone, and she was sure he wouldn't come back.

Not alone, anyway.

"Let me help you up," she said to the woman on the ground.

When the woman was on her feet, holding her dress together, she said, "Thank you."

"Sure."

The woman started from the alley, then turned and looked uncomfortably at Liz. She was dark-haired, young and pretty and, from what Liz had seen, had a fairly nice, firm body. For the first time Liz also noticed that she was Oriental, although she spoke perfect, accentless English.

"He was right, you know," the woman said. "I'm a whore."

Liz shrugged and said, "Even a whore deserves a day off every once in a while."

The woman smiled and said, "My name is Carla Lee."

"Liz Archer."

"Thanks again, Liz."

"Any time, Carla."

''If you need anything while you're in San Francisco, call on me and I'll see if I can help.'' She gave Liz an address on Sutter Street, and explained that it was the Barbary Coast and not exactly the best of areas.

''I'll remember.''

Carla Lee went to put herself back together, and Liz started back to the Alhambra for a bath. After that she donned her new outfit — admiring the way her orange bandana went with it (though she tucked it inside the collar) — and then went down to have dinner in the Alhambra dining room before hitting the gaming tables.

That was where she was when she came to the notice of Victor Drake.

Victor Drake had everything a man could want. He lived in San Francisco. He had power, money, possessions, successful businesses, everything he could possibly hope for — except a son to leave it to.

Oh, he had a son, all right. Vincent Drake, all of twenty-five, and every inch a weakling. All Vincent cared about was spending his father's money on gambling and whores, and he was not fit to inherit the Drake holdings.

Of course, Victor Drake enjoyed gambling himself, but he didn't throw money away as his son did. *He* gambled intelligently and won more than he lost.

Each of his evenings began with dinner at the Alhambra, followed by gambling, first at the Alhambra and then at one or two of the other gambling establishments in the square.

He was seated at his usual table, awaiting his order, when Liz Archer entered the dining room and caught his attention. And, of course, the attention of every other man in the room, even those already with a woman.

Vincent Drake entered the bordello on Ross Alley feeling confident and important, as he always did when he entered a whorehouse. Most of them knew who he was, and in this case the madam, Madam Chou, knew him better than most.

"Young Master," she greeted him, because she knew he liked to be called that.

"Madam."

"You will make a choice this evening?" she asked in stilted English.

"I will," he said. "Have them assemble in the sitting room."

The old madam bowed and said, "As you wish."

Liz entered the dining room knowing that she was drawing attention for several reasons. First, she was beautiful. She knew that, and it was not vanity to admit it.

Second, she was wearing her gun — probably the only woman in the room wearing one. She had opted for the pants this evening, and was wearing her gunbelt on her hip. *That* certainly drew attention, but she had never even entertained the thought of leaving the weapon in her room.

Third, she had the feeling that many of the people in the dining room were regulars, and she was both a stranger and a woman alone.

"Will you be dining alone, ma'am?" a waiter asked, approaching her.

"Yes."

He nodded and said, "Follow me, please."

"Who is that woman?" Victor Drake asked his waiter, Henry.

Henry looked over to the table where the blonde woman

was being seated and said, "I don't know, sir."

"See if you can find out, eh?" Drake asked.

"Yes, sir, Mr. Drake."

Drake liked women as much as his son did, and at forty-eight he was certainly not too old to enjoy them, but the type of women he enjoyed were entirely different from those his son chose.

Drake disdained whores.

He preferred high-class women, and that didn't mean women who thought they had class. That meant women like the blonde who had just been seated at a small table, the kind of woman who had class but either didn't know it or didn't care.

He waited patiently for Henry to come back and tell him who she was.

The dining room was full, and Liz knew that a lot of men — and women, too — were watching her. She particularly noticed the well-dressed man sitting alone, though, because he and she were the only two solitary diners. The other tables were mostly taken up by couples or foursomes, with an occasional threesome thrown in.

The man was watching her, and she knew that sooner or later he would make some kind of move. What she didn't know yet was how she would react.

After all, she was in San Francisco to relax and enjoy herself, and that would be a lot easier with the help of a man, wouldn't it?

Henry the waiter checked with the clerk on the desk, telling him that the information was for Mr. Drake. When the clerk heard that and listened to the waiter's description, he knew that only one person fitted the bill.

"She is registered as Elizabeth Archer," Henry told Victor Drake.

"From where?"

"She gave no address, sir."

"All right, Henry. Take her a bottle of champagne from me."

"Yes, sir."

When the waiter approached her table carrying the ice bucket and the bottle of champagne, Liz had no trouble figuring out who it was from.

"Compliments of Mr. Drake, ma'am," Henry said, putting the bucket down next to her table. "Would you like me to pour?"

"No," she said, and when the waiter gave her a puzzled look she added, "Not unless the gentleman will join me and help me drink it."

The waiter nodded and said, "I will check, ma'am."

"Thank you."

She watched the waiter walk to the man's table, exchange a few words and then start back. Behind him she saw the well-dressed gentleman stand up and also start for her table.

He was tall and slender and appeared to be in his forties. His dark hair was shot with gray. On his right hand he wore a diamond ring that glinted as he moved.

The man reeked of money, and if he was willing to spend some of it on Liz Archer, she wasn't going to argue.

The surprising thing was that he paid for her dinner and a couple of bottles of champagne and didn't try to take her to bed.

"It's been a lovely dinner, Miss Archer," he said. "And now it's time for me to do some gambling."

"I had intended to do some of that myself, Mr. Drake."

"I would ask you to accompany me, but I'm afraid you would be too much of a distraction, and I take my gambling very seriously."

He stook up, and she stared at him in surprise.

"I hope you don't mind?" he said.

"No," she said, finding her voice. "I don't mind at all."

"Perhaps we could have dinner again tomorrow evening?"

"I'd like that, Mr. Drake."

"Victor, please."

"Victor."

"Good night, Elizabeth," he said. "Good luck with your gambling."

"And with yours."

As the man walked out of the dining room Liz didn't know whether to be glad she hadn't had to fend off his advances — or insulted that he had not made any.

CHAPTER THREE

VINCENT DRAKE noticed the little Chinese girl right off, and she noticed him, too. He was conscious of her eyes following him everywhere as he strode about the sitting room, inspecting Madam Chou's girls.

Many of them were clad in diaphanous gowns, while others simply wore lingerie. The Chinese girl wore a neck-high red dress that was slit up to her thighs on both sides.

"I'll take her," Drake said, pointing to the Chinese whore.

"A fine choice, Young Master," Madam Chou said. "Ling?"

The Chinese girl responded to her name by rising and gliding toward Drake and the madam.

"This is Mr. Drake. You will be his for this evening."

"As you wish."

"Maybe for the night," Drake said.

The Chinese whore turned her limpid brown eyes on

him full force and said, "Anything you wish."

When she said that, Vincent Drake got an instant erection. Taking Ling by the arm, he led her to the stairway that went to the second floor, where all the girls had their rooms.

It was going to be quite a night.

The two men came out of the back room. As Drake climbed the stairs with the girl, the men crossed the room, ignored by Madam Chou's other girls. The men waited until they heard the door to Ling's room close and then started up the steps.

Inside the room, Drake watched Ling shed her dress. His eyes glittered when her brown-nippled breasts came into view, bobbing as she discarded her lingerie. When she was naked she came very close to him and asked huskily, "Would you like me to undress you?"

"Yes," Drake said, taking to the idea immediately.

She removed his coat, and his shirt, then unbuckled his pants and let them drop to his ankles. She reached into his shorts for his rigid member and began to lick it up and down, while he shivered and cupped her head in his hands. Moaning, she took the organ into her mouth. She sucked him lovingly, knowing that she had to keep his attention or forfeit her life. She brought him to the brink of orgasm, only to stop him before he could come. Then she started all over again.

Her job was to keep his attention, and that's what she was using her considerable skills to do.

She had no desire to die.

Wilkes turned the knob of the girl's door and opened it

silently. As he entered, he saw that Drake's back was to him. Drake's pants were down around his ankles, and the Chinese girl was in front of him, using her mouth to keep him busy. Her tiny hands were clutching the man's pale buttocks, her nails almost drawing blood, and Wilkes felt his own cock swelling inside his pants.

The man with Wilkes was called Hansen, and his favorite weapon was the bowie knife that had been made especially for him, which he now removed from the sheath on his hip. The blade was longer than most, almost like a short saber, so long that it would go right through a man as slender as Drake.

That's where the trouble started.

Hansen moved in behind Drake, who chose that moment to turn sideways a bit, holding onto the Chinese girl's head. Her eyes were open, and when she saw Hansen and his knife she spat out Drake's cock and gasped. Drake, sensing something wrong, started to turn, but Hansen drove his blade forward, piercing Drake's spine and driving through his body. The man gasped and fell to the floor, his rigid cock spurting his seed all over the floor.

Unfortunately, the Chinese whore chose that moment to stand up. As she did so, Hansen's blade came out from Drake's sternum and punched between her small breasts. She didn't even have time to scream.

When Hansen pulled his blade free — not without some effort — both Drake and the girl fell to the floor, dead.

"Shit," Wilkes hissed, shutting the door behind them. He checked both Drake and the girl and, finding them both dead, stood up. "Shit," he repeated.

He looked at Hansen. "The girl was supposed to get the blame," he said.

Hansen frowned and said, "Well, what do we do now?"

Wilkes thought quickly and then said, "We'll have to get another girl."

"I'll go down — "

"Not one of Madam Chou's," Wilkes said. "The boss won't wanna lose two girls in one night. We'll have to get someone else."

"From where?"

"I don't know," Wilkes said. "You stay here and don't let anyone in. I'll go out and find somebody."

"And then what?"

"Then we get rid of this body, substitute the other girl, move them to another place and let the police find her with the body. It'll work just the way the boss wanted it to. Just don't let anyone in until I get back!"

"All right."

Hansen replaced his knife, then looked down at the naked whore, whose body was still warm.

"Can I play with her?" he asked, licking his lips.

"Do whatever you want, Hansen," Wilkes said.

"All right!"

Wilkes went out the door into the hallway and made his way to the back stairway. He went out the back door and left it unlocked so he could get in again when he had found another girl. His best bet would be a stranger, and he knew where to go looking for one. He'd get another man to help him, and then they'd go where lots of strangers went when they came to San Francisco.

Portsmouth Square.

As soon as Wilkes had left, Hansen reached down and pulled the Chinese whore away from the dead man. Without bothering to put her on the bed he began to straighten her limbs eagerly . . .

For a short time, Liz noticed, Victor Drake stayed at the Alhambra to gamble, usually across the room from her. His concentration seemed complete, for he never once seemed to notice her. Later on in the evening she didn't see him any more and assumed that he had moved on.

Her own gambling was confined to some roulette and blackjack, although she was inexpert at both. It was just something to pass the time.

She was involved with losing her money, so she did not notice the two men who entered the place late and spotted her almost immediately.

Things might have been different if she had.

By about midnight Liz got tired of losing her money — although since she had not been betting big she hadn't lost very big. Still, she wanted to make sure her poke lasted her a while, so she decided to call it a night.

She wasn't followed upstairs, because the two men had already found out her room number and were waiting for her when she entered. Tate Gilmore, her mentor and probably the only man she had ever honestly cared about, would have given her hell for walking into it like that. It took one blow behind the ear with a balled fist, and she fell in slow motion, blacking out before her face hit the floor.

CHAPTER FOUR

THE RETURN OF consciousness brought bewilderment to Liz, all the more so because she had been struck down almost before she realized there was any danger.

Now, as her eyes fluttered open, she took a few moments to determine what had happened to her. Staring at the ceiling, she was aware that she had a headache that seemed to start behind her left ear. She also realized that she was lying on a hardwood floor. She'd had some champagne, sure, but not enough to have knocked her out. Something else had knocked her out and left her with a lump and a pounding behind that ear.

She must have been robbed.

She ran her hands over her body and found that she was naked. Had she been robbed and violated?

She probed between her legs but could find no evidence that she had been raped.

It was time to try and get up.

She braced her hands against the floor and pushed herself to a sitting position, closing her eyes against the pounding in her head. Once she was upright she opened her eyes to look around and study her surroundings.

She was not in her hotel room at the Alhambra, but in a room that looked as if it belonged to a much cheaper hotel. On second thought — as she looked around — it looked more like a crib, the kind prostitutes used when they couldn't afford to work the hotels or saloons.

A crib?

She looked around some more and saw the man lying on the pallet by the wall. Staggering to her feet she padded over to him and saw that he'd been skewered through the middle and was quite dead. The bleeding had stopped, so he'd been dead for some time.

What the hell was going on?

Her pounding head made thinking an effort, but after a while she decided that this felt like a frame and she couldn't afford to wonder about it now.

She looked around frantically and found her clothes. That confirmed her belief that it was a frame. If they had left her without clothes, the police would wonder what had happened to them.

She was dressed and looking for her gun when the police arrived and grabbed her.

Liz's only hope seemed to lie in the fact that Inspector Granger was taken with her. She could see that right off.

Two uniformed members of the San Francisco Police Department had broken in on her while she was searching for her gun and brought her before the inspector.

Granger seemed young for a man in authority, thirty-one or two, and as soon as she was led into his office she could see from his expression that he liked the way she looked. For that matter, he wasn't bad-looking, either. Tall and slim, he moved gracefully, coming around his desk to face her.

"Leave us alone," he told the two policemen.

"Yes, sir."

When they were gone he looked at her, and she stared back at him boldly.

"You don't look like a whore."

"I'm not," she said. "You don't look like a lawman."

"I am. What were you doing in that crib near the Barbary Coast?"

"Is that where it was?" she asked. "I don't know what I was doing there."

"Oh?"

"The last thing I remember I was entering my room at the Alhambra."

"And?"

"Someone knocked me out and took me to that crib."

"You're being framed?"

"Yes."

"Why? Do you have enemies in San Francisco?"

"No, I just got here today."

"Ever been here before?"

"No."

"Then why would someone want to frame you?"

"I don't know," she snapped, then tried to regain control of herself.

"Don't get upset."

"That's easy for you to say," she replied. "You're not being framed for murder."

"Did you know the dead man?"

"No."

"What did you do with the knife?"

"What knife?"

"The one you used to stab him."

"Don't get upset, you said?" Liz arched an eyebrow at him.

"Sorry," he said. "Just doing my job."

"I'm sure."

"Would you like a drink?"

"Hell, yes."

"Please, sit down," he said, and went back around his desk. He sat down himself and produced a bottle of whiskey and two glasses from his desk.

"Here," he said, handing her a glass with two fingers of whiskey in it.

After she had tossed it off he said, "Now tell it to me again."

"What?"

"All of it."

"Why?"

"I want to see if your story changes."

It didn't, not any of the five times she repeated it for him. It stayed the same, though not word for word, which was the reason she felt the man might have believed her. If it were a phony story she'd have memorized it and repeated it word for word each time.

"All right," he said, and she misunderstood.

"I can go?" she asked, standing up.

"No."

"Why?"

"You were found at the scene, Miss Archer," he explained. "I have to hold you."

"You don't have to," she asked. "Do you?"

"You're very beautiful," he said. "And you are certainly not a whore."

"Then why hold me?"

He studied her for a few moments, then shook his head, averted his eyes and said, "I have to. I'm sorry."

He went to the door for his two police officers and told them to take her to a cell.

"I'll be down to see you shortly," he told her. "I have to talk to my superiors."

"I'll have coffee ready," she said, and then left, accompanied by the two men who would take her to her new quarters.

"I understand she's extremely attractive," Police Chief Horace Steelman said.

"Word travels fast," Inspector Granger commented.

"Could that be the reason you believe her?" the chief went on, ignoring the remark.

"I don't think I deserve to be asked that question, Chief."

The chief studied the young man for a few silent moments. Steelman was an ex-Pinkerton's man who had been hired as chief of police to try and stem the growing crime wave that was spreading through Chinatown and the Barbary Coast. He was fifty-four now, and had vowed that after this job was through he'd retire. It had been he who had recruited Granger, also a former Pinkerton's operative, and promoted him over older men because he felt the young man was an excellent law officer.

"Maybe you're right," Steelman finally said. "Why do you believe her, then?"

"She's obviously not a whore, Chief," Granger said.

"Is that all?"

Granger ticked off points on the fingers of his right hand.

"She's registered at the Alhambra like she said. We found a gun and gunbelt in the crib, but no knife. Even if I believed that she had stabbed him, it wouldn't be with a blade like this. No woman could carry a blade like that hidden away."

"There's something else, too, isn't there?" Steelman asked.

"A couple of things," Granger said. "The body of a Chinese whore was found tonight, floating in the bay."

Steelman shrugged and said, "Another unlucky prostitute."

"Not just another one," Granger said. "She was stabbed, too. Run through with a large, thick blade."

Steelman frowned.

"Like the man?"

"Yes."

"What's the other reason?"

"I know of a man who carries a blade like that," the inspector said. "An extra-long bowie knife that he had made especially for him."

"Who?"

"His name is Hansen, and he hires out for . . . odd jobs."

"Like murder?"

"Like murder."

Steelman rubbed his lantern jaw and said, "What do you want to do?"

"I'm not sure," Granger said. "But I'd like your permission to do what I think is best."

Steelman thought it over for a moment, then decided that if he couldn't trust Granger with that much leeway he couldn't trust anyone.

"All right, but if you don't come up with something, we're gonna have to go with her. Understood?"

"Understood, Chief. Thank you."

When Granger didn't leave right away Steelman said, "Is there something else?"

Granger frowned and said, "Just a nagging feeling that I'm missing something here."

"Well, try to dredge it up in your own office, will you?" Steelman said.

"Yes, sir."

Granger was heading for the door — a little too quickly for Steelman's liking — when the chief called out, "Wait!"

"Sir?"

"Has the dead man been identified?"

"Uh, yes, sir."

"I thought so," Steelman said. "The way you were trying to get out of here before I asked, I'm afraid to hear this, but go ahead. Who was he?"

"Vincent Drake."

"Victor Drake's son?"

"Yes."

"Oh, shit," Steelman said, and Granger hurried out of his office.

Carla Lee was in love with Inspector Dan Granger, even though she knew that he, a lawman, could never love a whore. Still, that didn't stop him from sampling her charms from time to time, as he had done the previous night. It was then that she had told him about the woman who had helped her on the street, and that was why he had recognized Liz Archer when she was led into his office. It had nothing to do with the fact that she was Angel Eyes. He didn't know that . . . yet.

Granger left the police station and went to Carla Lee's apartment on Sutter Street.

"Dan," she said, backing up to allow him to enter. "I didn't expect you again so soon."

Granger didn't usually visit her two days in a row—not that she minded when he did.

"Are you alone?"

"You know I don't bring men to my room."

"*I'm* here on business, Carla," he told her as she shut the door behind them.

"Couldn't we talk about your business . . . after?" she asked.

She was wearing a blue dress, and she slid it from her shoulders so that her dark-nippled, firm breasts were bare, waiting for the touch of his hand or mouth. Already, her nipples were hardening. He was the only man who could make her feel this way after all her years of whoring.

"Business," Granger said, but since he couldn't take his eyes off her naked breasts he added, "first."

He knew how she felt about him and wished he could reciprocate, but he just didn't love her. He thought she was exotically beautiful, and he enjoyed being with her in bed. He knew that wasn't fair to her, but she seemed willing to accept only what he could give her.

"All right," she said, but did not cover her breasts. She crossed her arms beneath them, pushing them up, and said, "What kind of business?"

"I want you to do me a favor."

"What?"

"I want you to help someone escape from jail."

CHAPTER FIVE

THE LAST THING Liz Archer expected in jail that day was a visitor, but she got one.

Carla Lee.

After the guard had let Carla into her cell, Liz said, "How did you know I was here?"

"I heard," was all Carla would say. "You helped me yesterday, so now I'd like to help you." Today she was clothed much more sedately than yesterday, in a dress made high to the neck, though still somewhat tight and figure-revealing.

"How?"

The other woman reached beneath her skirt and produced a small gun, a two-shot derringer.

"What am I going to do with that?" Liz asked, almost laughing.

"For one thing, you could use it to get yourself a bigger gun,'' Carla said. ''After that you can get yourself out of here, and out of town.''

''That'd be an admission of guilt,'' Liz said. ''I'd be on the run for the rest of my life. No thanks, Carla. Take your little gun and go on back home. They can't prove I killed that man.''

''There's one other thing you could do, then,'' Carla said, still holding the gun out.

''What's that?''

''Get out of here and clear yourself. Nobody in this town is gonna do it for you.''

Liz had to admit that she was right on that count. She didn't know anyone in San Francisco but this soft-hearted whore, who couldn't do much more for Liz than she was doing right now.

''All right,'' Liz said, accepting the gun.

''Good.''

''Tell me something, Carla?''

''What?''

''Whose idea was this?''

''What do you mean?''

''It sure wasn't yours.''

''Why not?''

Liz looked at the girl and decided to stop pushing her. Whoever was behind this didn't want his — or her — identity known at the moment. Maybe once Liz was out her benefactor would come forward.

''All right, Carla,'' Liz said. ''You'd better get out of here now.''

''When are you gonna do it?''

''I don't know when,'' Liz said. ''When the time is right, I guess.''

Liz called for the guard and, before he arrived, said to Carla, "You tell whoever put you up to this that I'll want to talk to them before long."

"I don't know — "

"I know, you don't know what I'm talking about," Liz said as the guard approached. "Thanks, anyway."

On her way out, Carla stopped by Granger's office to tell him that the favor was done.

"I'll expect my payment later on," she added.

"I'll try to come by, Carla. When is she going to try it?"

"She said when the time was right," Carla replied, studying Granger critically. For the second time since he had come to her room she thought she detected that he was taking more than just a professional interest in Liz Archer. "She also said she's gonna want to meet you sooner or later."

"You didn't tell her — ?"

"No, I didn't tell her you sent me, but she knew it wasn't my idea."

"That's all right," Granger told her. "You did good, Carla."

Carla frowned and asked, "Why are you helping somebody break out of your own jail, Dan?"

"I'm just setting out a piece of bait, Carla," he said, "and waiting to see what snaps at it."

"That doesn't sound very fair."

"Thanks for the favor, Carla."

Carla Lee realized that he was telling her to keep her opinions to herself — and to leave. As she started for the door, however, he called her name.

"Yes?"

"Be a little careful, will you? One pretty china doll has already been killed."

"I'm touched by your concern, Dan," Carla said, "but in my business you don't make a living by staying indoors."

"How's your brother Harry?" Granger asked.

"Fine."

"Is he still running with the tong in Chinatown?"

Harry Lee, Carla's older brother, was a member of no great standing with the Black Hatchet Tong, and Granger had warned him that there was no future for him there. Granger often advised Carla to try and talk to Harry herself.

"Harry's got a mind of his own," Carla said.

With that she left, secretly pleased at the warning. At least it meant he cared . . . a little.

After Carla left, Dan Granger sat behind his desk and wondered why he was doing what he was doing. Sure, it had something to do with a dead Chinese whore and the dead son of an important man — each of whom was equally important to Granger. It also had to do with that little lady's blonde hair and blue eyes. Damned if she didn't have eyes just like . . .

Just like an angel.

"Angel Eyes," he said, slapping his palm down on his desk top so hard that his hand went numb.

Granger leaped out of his seat and hurried down to the jail, but by the time he got there, Liz Archer was gone.

"What happened?" he asked the guard, who was tied to a chair.

"Damned if I know," the man said, as Granger untied him. "She called me over, and when she showed me the barrel of that little gun I did whatever she said."

"She get her gun?"

"Yep," the man said, rubbing his wrists. "I wasn't about to deny that little lady anything that she wanted."

"Well, nobody ever said you were dumb, Roy," Granger said.

"Uh, are you gonna have to tell the chief about this?"

"I'll tell him something, Roy. Don't worry about it, just go back to work."

"Sure, Inspector. Thanks."

Now all Granger had to do was figure out how to tell the chief that he had allowed the infamous Angel Eyes to escape from their jail — with her gun!

Liz Archer went back to the Alhambra just long enough to pick up her gear and her horse. Then, for want of a better place to go, she rode to the Barbary Coast to find Carla Lee's Sutter Street address.

CHAPTER SIX

WHEN LIZ REACHED the Barbary Coast she saw how right Carla had been. It was quite different from Portsmouth Square, although much the same kinds of activities seemed to be going on. The saloons on Sutter Street and along the coast did not seem all that concerned about appearances, the way they did in the square.

Liz found a livery and paid in advance to put Blossom up for a few days. She had no idea how long it was going to take her to clear herself, so when the man told her she'd have to pay in advance, she simply pulled three days' worth of money out of her poke. If it took longer, she'd have to give him more money. This seemed to say something about the type of clientele the Barbary Coast drew.

She walked along Sutter Street then, looking for the number Carla Lee had given her, and had to sidestep more than one amorous drunk, which she did with little or no trouble. Many of them simply shrugged and moved on to the next woman.

She finally found Carla's building. On the ground floor it was a hardware store, but there was a stairway on the side, and she climbed up it to knock on the door.

"Liz!" Carla said in surprise when she opened the door. "Why, I just got back myself. You must have — "

"I didn't want to waste any time, Carla," Liz said. "May I come in?"

"Oh, of course," Carla said, backing away from the door. "Quickly, before someone sees you."

Liz stepped past the girl, who looked outside nervously and then shut the door firmly.

"I didn't have anywhere else to go," Liz said.

"That's all right. You're welcome here."

"I just need to get some rest so I can think straight."

"There's plenty of room on the bed, if you don't mind sleeping with me."

"No, I don't mind if you don't."

"It doesn't bother me," Carla said, shaking her head. "I've done more with other women than — well, never mind."

Carla had her lamp on low, and in the dim light Liz could see that she had not even had time to undress. She must have made a stop somewhere before coming home, probably to talk to whoever had put her up to giving Liz a gun.

"It's late," Carla said. "Why don't we get to bed and talk in the morning."

"That's fine with me."

Carla started to undress immediately, saying to Liz, "I think I can find a nightgown for you."

Liz began to undress, and soon both women were naked. Liz had never actually been with another woman before while they were both naked, and she frankly examined the other girl's body. Carla's breasts were smaller than Liz's, but high and firm, with dark nipples. Carla was smaller and slimmer than Liz, with a flat tummy and a nice behind, which Liz was able to see while the other girl rummaged through a bottom drawer for an extra nightie. Liz was further intrigued by the fact that the girl was Chinese. When the girl turned and caught Liz studying her, Liz felt herself flush and looked away.

"Don't be shy," Carla said, touching her arm. "You can look at me all you want. I'm not shy."

"I didn't mean — "

"I'll bet you're experienced with men, aren't you?" Carla asked.

"Yes, I suppose I am," Liz said. She wondered what Carla would think if she knew that much of her experience had been gained in a whorehouse.

"But not with women?"

Liz looked at Carla now and said, "You don't mean—?"

"Sure I do," Carla said, grinning. "I've taken money to be with men *and* women. It's really quite nice to be with another woman sometimes. I'm with so many men in my business that being with a woman is . . . like a night off. And I can let myself go and really feel!"

"I never . . . thought about . . . doing it . . . with another woman."

"I mean, men are best, of course," Carla said, "but a change is always nice. You have a beautiful body, Liz." Carla reached out to stroke the underside of one of Liz's breasts. Liz felt her heart begin to pound, but she did not pull away from the contact. Carla's fingertips felt very warm as they stroked her skin and then moved to her nipple. "Lovely nipples."

Liz admitted to herself that Carla was also lovely. Not as petite as most Chinese women, the girl had a flawless body, exotic almond-shaped eyes and long, inky-black hair parted down the center. Her hair fell down over her breasts, partially obscuring her brown nipples from view.

"Carla —" Liz said curtly as her nipple began to stiffen beneath the other girl's touch.

Carla pulled her hand away and said, "I'm sorry. Here," she added, handing Liz the nightie. "I hope you don't mind if I don't wear one, but on warm nights I like to sleep naked."

Both women were about the same age, and Liz was certainly not inexperienced in sexual matters, but for some reason Carla's casual attitude was making her feel awkward, as if she were a child and Carla was an adult who knew much more.

"It is warm, isn't it?" Liz said.

"You can sleep naked, too, if you like. It won't bother me — unless it bothers you, of course."

"Uh, no," Liz said, setting the nightie aside. "It doesn't bother me."

"All right, then. Let's go to bed."

"Sure."

Carla went to the bed and drew the covers down. Liz saw that it was a very big bed.

"Do you bring . . . customers up here?"

"Oh no," Carla said, as she finished getting the bed ready. "This is my home. Sure, I've had men up here, but not customers."

Carla got into bed but did not pull the sheet up over her.

"Too warm for covers," she said.

It seemed perfectly natural to her to be in the same room, even the same bed, with another woman. Liz scolded herself for being nervous. She willed her heart to stop pounding so hard, but it wouldn't. She also tried to keep herself from looking at Carla, but she couldn't take her eyes off the girl's breasts, or the triangle of fine hair between her legs. She had stroked herself there, but it had never occurred to her to stroke another woman . . .

Sliding into bed next to Carla it seemed to her that she could still feel the other girl's fingers on her breast, pulling lightly on her nipple.

"Good night," Carla said, turning on her side so that her behind was facing Liz. She hadn't turned the lamp completely down.

"Good night, Carla."

Liz turned on her side, in the same position as Carla, so that they were facing away from each other. She knew that she should be concentrating on her predicament, but she was increasingly aware of the heat that was emanating from Carla's body.

Carla shifted position, bringing her behind into contact with Liz's just slightly, and then moving away. Liz had no way of knowing whether it was deliberate or not, but her skin seemed to tingle from the contact.

"Liz?" Carla said. "Are you asleep?"

"No."

"Are you nervous?"

"Yes."

"There's no need," Carla said. Liz felt the other girl shift around on the bed, and then suddenly Carla's breasts were touching Liz's back, the nipples scraping her skin, they were so hard. She felt Carla's hand on the firm globes of her buttocks, rubbing lightly, sliding her fingers along the crack between Liz's buttocks.

"I'm curious," Carla said, her hand sliding along Liz's hip and thigh now. "Are you?"

Liz could barely hear herself above the pounding of her heart as she answered, "Yes."

"Good," Carla said, and her hand moved to Liz's belly, then upward until she was cupping one of her large breasts. "Turn onto your back," she whispered, and Liz obeyed.

"I wish my breasts were as large as yours," Carla said, running her palm first over one breast and then the other.

"Your breasts are . . . lovely," Liz said, looking at them.

"Do you really think so?"

"Yes," Liz said, and then reaching out she touched one and repeated, "Yes."

She ran her fingertips over the other girl's breast and found the skin incredibly smooth and soft. She cupped it in her hand, enjoying the way the nipple felt against her palm.

"This is crazy," she said in a low voice.

"No," Carla said. "It's natural."

Carla leaned over and gently kissed Liz's right breast, wetting the nipple with her tongue. She did the same to the left one, this time laving the nipple more avidly than before. Liz felt a rush from inside of her, a heat that seemed to center between her legs.

"It's natural," Carla whispered again, and this time she kissed Liz's mouth. Liz squeezed Carla's breast in her hand, and the girl moaned against her mouth. She felt Carla's tongue touch her lips and resisted only for a second before opening her mouth and allowing it to enter.

Carla's lips were soft, unlike any man's, and her tongue

seemed to know exactly where to go. Liz pushed her own tongue against it, squeezing Carla's breast harder, and she felt her bed partner's hand snake down over her belly, tug at the golden hair between her legs, and then stroke her wet lips with a feather-light touch.

She moaned into Carla's mouth, and the girl lifted her thigh and draped her leg over Liz's. Her fingers, very knowing, very experienced, dipped into her and gently but firmly brought her to an orgasm, albeit a small one. It was like a tremor that ran through her body quickly, leaving her breathless, but wanting more.

"Liz," Carla said. "I'm sorry . . ." As if this were all her doing.

"Don't be," Liz said as Carla's mouth trailed down over her neck to her breasts. "Don't," she said as the other woman's lips began to run over her breasts.

When Carla fastened her mouth onto one nipple and began to suck it, Liz brought her hands up to cup the girl's head and hold it there. Carla's black hair smelled clean and fresh, and her mouth was eager on both breasts now, biting and sucking Liz's nipples until they were almost painfully erect.

"Liz . . . me," Carla said breathlessly. She hiked herself up so that her hot, sticky pussy was pressed against Liz's stomach and her firm little tits were dangling in Liz's face.

It seemed natural for Liz to lick them and then suck them, cupping them in her hands and holding them to her mouth like some overripe fruit.

"Oooh, yes," Carla said, and she was rubbing her oozing cleft against Liz's stomach until a tremor passed through her, as well.

They kissed again, giggling like kids against each other's mouths and tongues, until Carla said, "I'm ready for the big one. Are you?"

"Yes," Liz heard herself say.

Carla was on top of her now, her mouth still avid, her breasts pressed against Liz so that their nipples were scraping, and their pussies were rubbing urgently together. Both women were moaning and crying out against each other's mouths, and then they each stiffened as their orgasms overtook them, their cries mingling in the dim light.

"Are you . . . disgusted with me?" Carla asked a little later.

"No."

"With yourself?"

"No," Liz said, and she discovered that she was telling the truth. It had been a marvelous experience, although one that she would previously have thought of as . . . unnatural.

"I'm glad," Carla said.

They were lying side by side, a faint sheen of perspiration on their bodies, and Carla propped herself up on an elbow so she could look down at Liz.

"I want us to be friends."

"We are."

"Almost like sisters," Carla said, running her finger between Liz's breasts and down over her belly until it was between her legs.

"Not quite," Liz said, closing her eyes.

"We don't have to do anything else tonight," Carla said. "If you'd rather think about your problem — "

"I'd rather not," Liz said.

"Good," Carla said.

Liz opened her eyes as Carla shifted on the bed, and

suddenly the other girl's face was between Liz's legs. Liz tensed when she first felt the touch of Carla's tongue, but then relaxed and enjoyed it as Carla licked up and down the length of her slit, probing inside every so often, until she fastened her attention on Liz's swollen clit. As the Oriental girl expertly drove her toward a shattering climax, Liz wondered what it would be like to do that to another woman.

She soon found out.

Abruptly, Carla changed her position so that, although her mouth was still in the same place, her own slit was now hovering above Liz's mouth. Liz hesitated a mere second, then flicked out her tongue to taste her partner's wetness. Finding it interesting, she delved even deeper with her tongue until finally they both shuddered and came together. After which, they fell into a pleasantly exhausted sleep.

In the morning, they woke in each other's arms, exchanged a chaste kiss and then began to laugh.

"You were right," Liz told Carla while they dressed.

"About what?"

"Men are the best," she answered, "but a change is nice once in a while."

"I'm glad," Carla said. "Let's go and have some breakfast, and we can talk about your problem."

Liz was surprised at herself, at how good she felt after a night of sex with another woman, but it had been a new experience for her, and she enjoyed new experiences.

On the whole, she thought this was one she wouldn't mind repeating from time to time.

CHAPTER SEVEN

OVER BREAKFAST in a small cafe on the Barbary Coast Liz
tried to get Carla to reveal who had put her up to slipping
Liz the gun. In spite of what the two women had shared
the previous night, however, Carla would not talk.

"I can't," she said. "Please, Liz, don't ask me. I think
you'll find out soon enough, anyway."

"All right," Liz said, giving in.

"What will you do now?"

"Try and find out who I'm supposed to have killed."

"I can tell you that."

"You can? Who was he?"

"His name was Vincent Drake."

"*Vincent* Drake?" Liz asked, wanting to be sure she
had heard right.

"Yes. Did you know him?"

"I never met him," Liz said, "but I did meet a Victor
Drake."

"His father," Carla said, "and a very important man in this town. Some people think he's going to run for governor."

"Well, I'm sure a man like that has a lot of enemies who might have wanted to kill his son to get to him," Liz said. She added thoughtfully, "I don't have a motive for this murder, Carla."

"Maybe not," Carla said. "But you were there, and the police don't have anyone else."

"I've got to get them someone else, then."

"How are you going to do that?"

"I'll have to talk to Victor Drake and convince him of my innocence. Once I get him on my side he and I can figure out who the real murderer is."

"How will you get him to see you?"

"Do you know where he lives?"

"Yes," Carla said, and told Liz where and how to get there.

"I'll go there — "

"What if the police are watching his home?"

"I'll be careful," Liz said, wiping her mouth with a napkin and preparing to stand up.

"Would you like me to come along?"

"No, Carla, you've done enough."

"Will you come back to my place?"

"I'd rather find a hotel somewhere where I can hole up if I have to."

Carla stared at Liz for a few moments, and then mentally shrugged, figuring it was just as well. She didn't want to get used to having Liz around, and she was sure that Liz felt the same way.

"All right. Come back to my place and I'll take you

some place where they know me. Nobody will bother you while you're there.''

"All right.''

Carla took a key out of her purse and handed it to Liz.

"If I'm out just let yourself in and wait for me.''

Liz took the key with one hand and covered Carla's hand with the other.

"If you do need some help, Liz, I have a brother who would be willing to help you. Just let me know.''

"I don't know how I'll repay you, Carla.''

"Don't worry about it,'' Carla said, averting her eyes. "I'll see you later.''

Liz stood up, put some money on the table for the breakfast, and went out. She had left her saddlebags back at Carla's room, and figured they'd be safe there until she returned.

Carla left just moments later, on her way to meet with Inspector Dan Granger.

Dan Granger was nervously awaiting Carla Lee's arrival at his home. He had two rooms above a store on Market Street, and not many people knew where he lived. Steelman, of course, Carla, and some other street contacts, contacts he trusted more than his fellow law officers, many of whom were on the take from the Barbary Coast saloons and Chinatown gambling dens and whorehouses.

Granger was nervous because Liz Archer—Angel Eyes, damn it! —had escaped even faster than he had expected, and he hadn't had time to put a man on her tail. He could only hope that she *would* go to Carla, and that Carla would then come to him.

The knock on his door was tentative, the kind of knock

a person uses who doesn't really want the door to be opened.

It was Carla, and he sensed that something was wrong as soon as she entered.

"Carla?"

The girl looked at him.

"Well, did she come to your room?"

"Yes."

"And spend the night?"

"Yes. We had breakfast together."

"Where did she go from there?"

"I—" Carla began, then stopped herself short. "I don't know," she said finally, and Granger didn't believe her.

"You two become friends in a few hours?"

"Maybe."

"So now you're forgetting that we're friends, too?"

"Is that what we are?" Carla asked. "I thought I was just a whore you fucked sometimes."

"Carla, that not fair —"

"She's not guilty, Dan."

"Did I say she was? Would I have let her out if I thought so?"

"Tell her, then. She's going to get killed walking around being your bait."

"If you don't tell me where she went, I can't help her, Carla."

"Steelman wants to pin it on her, doesn't he?"

Granger thought back to his meeting with Steelman that morning. The chief had been visited earlier by Victor Drake himself, and Drake was demanding an arrest. Steelman had promised him one, and then had ordered Granger to go out and find Liz Archer again. It didn't make the Chief of Police any happier to hear that the woman they'd *had* in jail had herself a reputation for killing men.

"With a gun," Granger pointed out.

"So now she's found herself a new weapon," Steelman replied. "Find her, Granger, and get her back in that cell!"

Granger looked at Carla now and said, "Carla?"

Carla decided that she owed Liz at least a little bit of a head start.

"She'll be coming back to my room tonight," she told Granger.

"To stay?"

Carla shook her head.

"I'm taking her to Zeke's."

Zeke Mandel owned a run-down hotel on the Barbary Coast, and Granger knew from some of his street contacts that it was a sort of haven for people on the run.

"All right, then," Granger said. "If you can't tell me where she'll be before then . . . "

"She didn't say."

Granger knew that Carla was lying, but he let it pass, because he thought he knew where Liz Archer would go first.

To the father of the man she was supposed to have killed.

"I have to leave," he said, picking up his jacket. He slid it on over the shoulder rig he wore, with a cut-down .44 under his left arm.

"Sure," Carla said. "I have an appointment, anyway."

"A customer?"

"Yes," she said, lifting her chin and glaring at him defiantly. "A customer. A girl has to make a living."

"Everybody has to make a !living," Granger said, and

they left his rooms together, going their own ways once they hit the street.

Wilkes and Hansen were in the office of their employer, who was not happy.

"Things did not go exactly as planned, did they?" he asked.

"Uh, not exactly, sir," Wilkes said.

"There was nothing in the papers about Drake being killed by a whore," the man said. "Why is that?"

"I don't know, sir," Wilkes said. "She was in the room when the police got to the crib — "

"Crib?" his boss asked, looking confused. "What crib? You mean he wasn't found at Madam Chou's?"

That was when Wilkes explained exactly what had happened, while Hansen sat stolidly, not looking at either man. Hansen would start paying attention when they began to talk about giving him his money.

"This man?" their employer asked when Wilkes was finished with his story.

"Yes, sir."

The man stared at Hansen, who did not look back at him, and then shook his head.

"All right, so you did get a girl to take the blame. What happened to her?"

"I don't — "

"Well, find out, damn it!"

"Yes, sir."

Wilkes rose to leave, but Hansen remained seated.

"And take him with you."

Hansen finally looked at the man behind the desk and said evenly, "I don't leave until I get paid."

"Paid? For botching the job?"

"I always get paid when I kill somebody," Hansen said. "Otherwise, I do another one . . . for free."

When Wilkes and Hansen left, the killer had a lot more money than he had when he went in.

It took Liz Archer some time to find Victor Drake's residence on Nob Hill—time enough for Granger to get word to his men there to fade into the background and make sure they weren't seen . . . by anyone!

Orange bandana tucked inside her collar and blonde hair tucked underneath her hat, Liz cautiously approached the Drake house. It was a huge house, built of stone and stucco and hidden behind a thick wall of hedges. After watching for a while, Liz decided that the only way to get in was to walk to the front gate and announce herself. Once inside she knew she might find it hard to get out again, but she had to give it a try. Victor Drake was a powerful man, and he'd make a much better ally than he would an enemy.

CHAPTER EIGHT

"WHO?" Victor Drake asked.

"A woman . . . "

"I don't want to see anyone, George," Drake told his black houseman.

"She said you might say that, sir," George replied. "She says that you and she shared some champagne the other night, and that she wanted to talk to you about . . . your son."

Drake looked up from his desk and frowned at George, then shrugged and said, "Very well, let her in."

"Yes, sir."

When the houseman re-entered the office with Liz Archer, Victor Drake stook up.

"Miss Archer, to what do I owe this pleasure?"

"I heard about your son," Liz said. "I'm sorry . . . "

She was feeling awkward because she didn't know how much Drake knew about her involvement with his son's death — as negligible as she knew that involvement was.

"Thank you. Will you have a drink?"

Was he offering her a drink feigning ignorance to keep her there until the police arrived? There was only one way to find out.

"Mr. Drake, I assume you've spoken to the police about your son's death?"

"I have," Drake said, pouring two snifters of brandy from a crystal decanter, "and they've assured me that an arrest will be made."

Liz took the brandy and said, "I'm sorry, but you don't seem very upset about your son's death."

"I am, in my own way," he said. "But my son was . . . not what I had hoped for. He was weak, and he had disgusting habits, friends and . . . appetites. I knew he'd get himself killed sooner or later."

Still confused about his attitude, Liz asked, "Was there anything in the newspaper about his death?"

"Yes."

"They didn't mention anything about an arrest being made?"

"Only that one was imminent."

"Mr. Drake," she said, putting the brandy down, "I have something to tell you that you may not like."

"Oh?" He frowned at her. "What?"

"I was . . . with your son when the police found him."

"You?" he said disbelievingly. "You were in Portsmouth Square that evening. That's not — wasn't — my son's area. Besides, you're not his type."

"Nevertheless, I was found with him, arrested and put in a cell."

"I don't understand. If that's true, what are you doing here?"

"I escaped."

"Am I to believe that?"

"Please," Liz said. "Let me explain exactly what happened."

"I wish you would."

She told him the story of how she had returned to her room and been struck down, only to wake up in a crib on the Barbary Coast, with the dead body of his son nearby. She went on to explain how she was questioned and locked up, and how she came to escape.

"And then I came to see you. Now, you might be keeping me here until the police arrive, but I decided before coming that I'd have to take that chance."

"Why?"

"I need your help. I didn't kill your son. And I believe that between us we might be able to figure out who did."

"And clear yourself?"

"Yes."

"Well," he said, thoughtfully, "I haven't sent for the police because I knew nothing of your involvement."

"And now?"

George, the houseman, was still standing by the door, so Drake looked at him and said, "George, leave us alone. Tell Delores we'll have a guest for lunch, and if the police should come to the gate for any reason, don't let them in. Tell them I'm too distraught to talk to them."

"Yes, sir."

George left the room, which appeared to Liz to be a study, or library. The walls were lined with books, and there was a large oak desk almost in the center of the room.

"Now then," Drake said, "will you have another brandy while we try to figure this thing out together?"

"Why not?"

"Is she inside?" Granger asked his man, Joe Dunn.

"Yes, sir."

"Did you get my message?"

Granger had sent one of his street runners to the Drake house ahead of Liz Archer to tell Joe Dunn to send the rest of the men back to headquarters, but to remain himself.

"I did. I sent the others away."

Joe Dunn was one of Granger's men, one of only a handful that Granger really trusted.

"Do I get to know what's going on?"

"We want the girl and Mr. Drake to spend some time together."

Dunn looked at Granger and asked, "Does he know that she killed his son?"

"No," Dan Granger said, staring straight ahead at the house, "and neither do we."

CHAPTER NINE

LIZ ARCHER had not expected their discussion to take them from the lunch table to Victor Drake's bed, but that was exactly what happened.

Drake was on top of her, and he was deep inside her, his long, rigid penis sliding in and out of her, driving her toward a delicious orgasm. His hands were cupping her firm buttocks, holding her tightly against him so that when he slid back into her he achieved maximum penetration.

Drake was still in his physical prime, with the body of a man ten years younger than his forty-eight, and Liz had never had anything against older men. On the contrary, she found that they were seldom in as much of a hurry as younger men, since they had less to prove.

Liz knew another reason she might have gone willingly to Victor Drake's bed. Possibly she'd wanted to reaffirm her femininity after spending the night in Carla Lee's bed.

Whatever the reason, it was a very enjoyable experience.

As Drake continued to drive into her, squeezing her buttocks so hard they hurt, she wrapped her legs around him, bracing her heels against his behind. His pace was increasing, and soon he was slamming into her, yet still not hurrying. He was a man who had obviously had a lot of experience with women, and Liz was reaping the benefits of all that experience.

She sensed her orgasm approaching, and she could feel him swelling inside her. Knowing that he was waiting for her, she said, "Now, Victor, oh now!"

"Why did you bring me up here?" Liz asked afterward. Drake had simply risen from his seat opposite her, taken her by the hand and led her to his bedroom.

"I could tell you that I simply wanted to assure you that I don't suspect you of my son's murder."

"But — "

"But that wouldn't be true." Drake propped himself up on an elbow, looked down at Liz's face and said, "I simply wanted you. I looked across the table at you downstairs, and I wanted you."

"And there was no gambling to get in your way."

"I apologized for that the other night."

"I know you did," she said, stroking his strong-jawed face. "I was teasing."

If Drake had a fault it was that he seemed to take everything at face value. Still, that had probably worked to her advantage, because he had almost immediately believed in her innocence.

"I'm . . . not used to being teased."

"I'll try not to do it again."

"No, don't change," he said, sliding his hand up her

ribcage to cup one of her breasts. "Don't ever change."

"We have to talk," she said, taking that hand in both of hers.

"Later," he said.

"About your son's murder."

"You will find that I had very little regard for my son, and so have even less regard for his killer."

"But I want to prove that I'm not that person."

"You don't need to prove it to me."

"Maybe not; but to the police I do. The only way I'm going to do that is to find out who did kill him."

"All right," Drake said, drawing his hand from between hers. "We'll talk about it" — he slid his hand down between her legs — "later."

She was about to protest, but his index finger suddenly entered her, and she caught her breath. He bent his head and began to lick her nipples, and she closed her thighs over his hand, trapping it between them.

Before she knew it he had forced her legs apart gently, mounted her and entered her once again, taking her in long, easy strokes.

True to his word, these were not the actions of a distraught man.

In order to discuss the situation they finally had to take the subject out of the bedroom and back down to Drake's study.

"Who would have a reason to kill your son?"

"That would depend on a lot of things," Drake said.

"If we answer one question it would probably make things a lot easier."

"What question is that?"

"Was he killed because of something he did," Liz asked, "or something you did?"

Outside, Granger began to fidget as the time moved on toward dinner.

"What the hell are they doing in there?" he asked aloud.

Dunn glanced at Granger with a funny expression on his face and said, "Did you get a good look at that woman?"

"Sure I did," Granger said. "She was in my office."

"Then how could you ask that question? What do you think they're doing in there?"

For some reason, Dan Granger didn't want to think about that.

"Does a name come to mind, Victor?"

"Of course," Drake said. "Edward Simonson."

"Who is he?"

"I guess you'd say he was my rival, in almost every way," Drake said. "Mainly, he's my business rival and would do anything to try and ruin me."

Liz had the impression that their main rivalry was much more personal than that, but didn't ask about it just yet.

"Would killing your son help to do that?"

"No," Drake replied frankly. "But he might think it would."

"Did he know your son?"

"Oh, he knew him, all right," Drake replied. "He wanted his daughter to marry my son."

"Really?"

"It was a ploy to try and get inside my business."

"And what did your son think?"

"He wasn't interested in Gabrielle Simonson."

"Why not?"

Drake looked her right in the eye and said, "Because she's not a whore. My son believed in finding his pleasures beneath his station — and the further the better."

"Well, I suppose my next move is to talk to the Simonsons."

"Simonsons?" Drake said, questioning the use of the plural.

"Well, maybe Gabrielle was insulted. Women have killed for less reason."

"Is that a fact?"

"And so have men," she added.

She put her brandy glass down and stood up, preparing to leave.

"You'd better wait," Drake said, walking toward her.

"For what?"

"I'll have George check around outside and see if there are any police."

"If they're out there it's because they didn't want to come in and get me," Liz reasoned. "And if that's the case, then they're out there to follow me."

"Why? If they thought you were guilty they'd simply arrest you. Why follow you?"

"I don't know," she said, "but I guess there's only one way to find out."

"Will you come back here . . . tonight?"

"I have a place to stay for a while," Liz said, remembering Carla's offer to take her to a hotel. At the moment she thought that it would be wise to stick to her original plan.

After all, Victor Drake was constantly pointing out how much he disliked his son — and fathers have been known to kill their sons.

Drake told Liz where Simonson's office was and gave her directions on how to get there.

"It'll be dark soon," he reminded her.

"I know. I'll get off the streets before it gets too late."

"You'll come back and let me know what progress you've made?"

"If I find out who killed your son, Victor, I'll certainly let you know."

"Wait — " he said as she started from the room.

"What is it?"

"There's something else you should know."

"What?"

"I have . . . another son, and a daughter."

She turned to face him. "Why tell me now, if you had no intention of doing so before?"

"I want you to know everything," he said. "My son David is older than Vincent, and my daughter Vivien is the youngest. David is twenty-seven. Viv is twenty-three."

"They don't live here with you?"

"No," Drake said, looking as if it pained him to discuss them. "They live somewhere else . . . together." He gave her the address.

"Now that Vincent is dead, will you change your will?"

"I don't know," he said. "I was considering changing it while he was alive."

"In what way?"

"I was going to cut them all out," he said, frowning. "I'm not very proud . . . of any of them."

"Why?"

"Since you're going to be asking questions and meeting them, I'll let you find that out for yourself. Be very careful, Liz."

"I'll be careful with your children, Victor — "

He took hold of her arms and said, "I'm more concerned with your welfare, Elizabeth. Take care."

"I will."

"I'll help in any way I can."

"I appreciate that, Victor," she said, "but considering
how you feel about your son, this is really my problem."

"Considering how I feel about you," he said, "I'm making it mine, also."

She smiled her thanks, kissed him and left. George led
her to a door at the back of the house and wished her luck.

CHAPTER TEN

EDWARD SIMONSON'S OFFICE was on Kearny Street, in a section of San Francisco known for its expensive shops. The section also housed the offices of some fairly large businesses.

Simonson's was one of the largest.

Liz saw no less than three buildings displaying the Simonson name — shipping, mining and agricultural businesses.

In which building, she wondered, would she find Edward Simonson?

The only way to find out was to enter one and ask for him.

As she approached the building that housed Simonson Shipping she wondered if there was a policeman on her trail — and if so, why?

Something occurred to her then, something that she

wanted to ask Carla about, but that would have to wait till later.

As she entered the building she saw that it contained both office and warehouse space. She was sure that Simonson would have an even larger warehouse down by the docks.

After a few moments it also became evident that the work day at Simonson's was over and that her trip had been wasted.

Or had it?

She was about to give up when a young man exited from one of the offices, locking the door behind him. When he turned and saw her he stopped short and they examined each other.

He was tall, with broad shoulders that looked out of place inside his business suit. He looked as if he'd be more at home in range clothes. His hair was dark and thick, and his chin had a deep cleft in it. She had to admit that he was an extremely good-looking man. He also seemed impressed with her.

We'd make a handsome couple for sure, she couldn't help thinking, in spite of the fact that he seemed to be only about nineteen.

"Hello," he said, finally breaking the silence.

"Hello."

"Can I help you?"

"I was looking for Edward Simonson."

He approached her and stopped a few feet away. "He's not here right now. Can I help you with something?"

"Who are you?"

"My name is Simonson. Thomas Simonson. Edward is my uncle . . . and my boss." The last part was said with a noticeable lack of enthusiasm.

"You look like you belong on a horse, not in a suit."

He grinned, deepening the cleft in his chin even more. "You're right. I love riding, but Uncle Edward wants me to get involved with the business, so . . ." He shrugged, and his voice trailed off.

"And Gabrielle?"

"My cousin? She has no head for business at all. Do you know Gabby?"

"No."

"Uncle Edward?"

"Never met him."

Thomas Simonson frowned. "I don't think I understand."

"Can you tell me when your uncle will be here?"

"Some time tomorrow. He usually splits his time between businesses. You might find him at home tonight . . . but then you wouldn't know where he lives, would you?"

"No," she said. "And you wouldn't tell me, would you?"

"Not unless I get some sort of explanation out of you."

"Maybe another time, Thomas," she said, taking a backward step toward the door.

He looked at the gun on her hip, then said, "Couldn't we talk some more? Perhaps over dinner?"

"I'm sorry, I have a previous engagement."

"Maybe another time?" he asked as she reached the door.

She grinned at him and said, "Yes, maybe another time."

In fact, she even found herself looking forward to it — and more.

CHAPTER ELEVEN

WHEN LIZ GOT BACK to Carla's room, the other girl wasn't there. Liz let herself in. Carla was her friend now — and maybe more — and perhaps when she returned Liz would be able to get her to open up.

Especially since she had a theory now that she wanted to try out on her new friend.

While waiting she hung her gunbelt on the bedpost, lay down on the bed and promptly fell asleep. Some time later, the creaking of the door woke her. She lay perfectly still, poised to grab for her gun. Opening her eyes a crack she peered through the darkness and made out the silhouette of someone entering and closing the door.

"Liz?"

It was Carla.

"Here."

Carla paused to turn the lamp up until it glowed dimly, then moved to the bed and put her hand on Liz's arm.

"Are you all right?"

"I'm fine."

Carla smiled with relief. "Good."

"Carla," Liz said, easing her hand away from the other girl's touch, "I have to talk to you."

"You want me to take you to the hotel?"

"After we talk."

Carla sat on the bed. "About what?"

Liz got up from the bed and moved across the room.

"The man who told you to slip me that gun — " she began.

"I can't tell you — "

"You don't have to," Liz said. "*I'll* tell *you*. It was Inspector Granger, wasn't it?"

"How . . . did you know that?"

"It occurred to me today while I was on Kearny Street. He heard my entire story — five times. While I was telling it to him I had the feeling he believed me, but that his hands were tied. He had to put me in that cell; but I think he also wanted to help me out."

"Why?"

"I don't know," Liz said. "I can't figure that part. I think he might have someone following me, but why — ?"

"You're the bait."

"Bait?" Liz asked.

"That's what he said."

"Then he knows I'm not guilty. He's hoping that when the killer sees me free he'll try and get rid of me. When I'm dead, Granger won't be able to prove either that I killed Vincent Drake or that I didn't."

"Why doesn't he just let you go?"

"He's got to answer to his chief, Carla," Liz explained. "While I'm alive he has to try and solve this murder.

Victor Drake is an important man in San Francisco."

"You're telling me."

"The Chief of Police must be more than a little nervous. Granger's doing what he thinks is right, I'm sure of it."

"You approve of what he's doing?" Carla asked. "I don't understand either one of you."

"Why did you agree to help him?"

"Because I was helping you at the same time," Carla said. "I owed you that."

"And?"

"And . . . Granger and I are . . . friends," Carla said, avoiding Liz's gaze.

Liz had the feeling that Carla had said "friends" for want of a better word.

"Maybe you should take me to that hotel now," Liz said, crossing the small room and retrieving her gunbelt.

"Do you know how to use that?" Carla asked, watching from the bed as Liz strapped the gun on.

Liz smiled and said, "I know."

Carla stood up. "You could stay here again tonight, you know."

"I think I'd better go to the hotel, Carla. I hope you understand."

"I understand," Carla said. "Come on, before Inspector Dan Granger decides to show up and put you back in a cell — the bastard!"

Liz picked up her saddlebags and followed Carla from the room.

CHAPTER TWELVE

CARLA HAD DESCRIBED the hotel she called Zeke's as a dump, and Liz found that an apt description. It was on a darkened side street near the docks, and unless you knew where you were going you would never have thought it was a hotel.

"Do they do much business?"

"Not the kind that most hotels do," Carla said, pushing the door open. "You can check in here and do just about anything, and no one will bother you . . . as long as you can pay."

"How much — ?"

"You won't have to pay," Carla said as they stepped into the lobby. "I'll tell Zeke you're a friend of mine."

They walked to the front desk in the dimly lit lobby, and Carla tapped the bell once. A thin man stepped out from behind some ragged curtains. He fit right in with the surroundings. His face was covered with a dark stubble, which he scratched at while inspecting the two women. He appeared to be in his thirties, but Liz couldn't be sure.

"Carla."

"I need a room, Zeke."

Zeke looked at Liz and asked Carla, "For the two of you, for the night?"

"No, it's not like that," Carla said. "This is my friend, and she needs a place to stay."

"Sure," the man said. He turned to a pegboard, took down a key and held it out. "Room five. It overlooks the street."

"That's fine," Liz said, taking the key. "Do you want me to sign the register?"

He grinned, revealing a row of uncared-for teeth and said, "What register?"

Liz looked at Carla, who flicked her head toward the stairs.

"Payment in the usual way?" the man asked Carla, grinning.

"Don't worry," Carla said. "You'll get paid."

When they were upstairs in the hall, which was even dimmer than the lobby, Liz asked, "What did he mean, payment in the usual way?"

"Don't worry about it," Carla told her. "Zeke and I have an arrangement."

"Are these other rooms occupied?"

"Some. You'd better get inside and get some rest. I have to go."

"To see Granger?"

"I'm supposed to report to him."

"He probably had someone follow me, Carla. He knows where I am."

"I'll talk to him and see if he'll help you, Liz," Carla said, as Liz used the key to unlock the door. She noticed that although the door was old, the lock was new.

"You don't have to do that — "

"We're friends, aren't we?" Carla said, cutting her off.

"Yes."

"Well, I don't have that many real friends, Liz. Let me help the one I have, all right?"

Liz smiled. "All right."

"I'll see you here tomorrow."

"I have to go out — "

"I'll check in once in a while to see if you're here. If you need anything, just tell Zeke."

"Thanks, I will."

"Good night."

Liz entered the room and closed the door behind her. She turned up the lamp next to the door just enough so that she could see. The room was small, with a rickety bed, a chair and a small table. When she sat on the bed she found that although the frame was unsteady, the mattress was good. The clientele here obviously had need of locks and mattresses.

She made good use of them both.

When Carla went downstairs she walked around the desk and through the torn curtains. On the other side Zeke was sitting on a pallet against the wall, naked, a dreamy look on his face. His hand was between his legs, stroking his long, thin penis, which was ragingly erect. Carla moved toward him, got down onto her knees between his legs and went about making payment for the favor in the usual way.

Outside, Joe Dunn settled into a doorway for what he assumed would be the night. If the blonde left he'd follow;

if the Oriental girl left he'd stay and watch for the blonde.

Those were his orders, and Joe Dunn always followed orders. He couldn't help thinking, though, about those good-looking women, probably both warming beds inside, while he stayed outside, chilled by the cold air coming off the bay.

He could sure use a warm woman right about now.

Once again Wilkes and Hansen were in their employer's office, and he was still not happy. He was not happy that Hansen was still with Wilkes, and he was less than pleased with what Wilkes had just told him about the blonde whore.

"Why has she been set free if she was found on the scene?" he demanded.

"I don't know, sir," Wilkes said. "Apparently, the investigation is still going on."

"Who's in charge?"

"Inspector Granger."

"Damn," his employer swore. "That man can't be bought!"

"No, sir."

The man behind the desk looked at Hansen. To Wilkes he said, "Is this man still willing to . . . work?"

"Yes, sir."

"For payment in advance," Hansen added.

"Of course."

"Granger?"

"No, fool. As long as the blonde whore is alive, Granger has a chance of proving her innocent. Once she's dead, that chance vanishes. He won't be able to prove her innocent — or guilty. I'd prefer that situation to the one that presently exists. Do you get my meaning?"

"Yes, sir."

"All right, then," the man said, his annoyance clearly etched on his face. He opened his top desk drawer, took out two packets of money and tossed one to each man.

"Get it done, then — and do it right, this time."

Liz lay awake for a while thinking about Drake and Granger and Carla Lee. She thought about Drake's other two children, whom he seemed even less proud of than he had been of Vincent. In fact, when he had spoken about them the look on his face had been one of disgust.

Had Vincent Drake been killed by his father, by his brother or sister or by someone outside of the family?

It didn't really matter, she realized, because the important thing to prove was that *she* had not done it. According to Carla, Granger knew that, but he still had his chief to answer to.

Tomorrow, she decided, she had to have another meeting with Granger. She'd ask Carla to set it up, although the girl had done quite enough for her already.

At last she drifted off to sleep. She dreamed that she was in a huge bed with Victor Drake and Carla Lee. Neither one was paying any attention to her.

Wilkes and Hansen sat at a table in a bar on the Barbary Coast. There were a few gaming tables around the room — and fewer clean glasses. It was about as far removed from the Alhambra and other Portsmouth Square establishments as it could be.

"How are we going to find her?" Hansen asked Wilkes. "We can't check every hotel in San Francisco."

"We won't have to," Wilkes said. "All we have to do is find Granger and keep an eye on him. He's investigating her, and sooner or later he'll find her for us."

"And then I'll take care of them both at the same time," Hansen said, sliding his wicked blade halfway out of its leather sheath.

"You can't kill a lawman!" Wilkes said to him in a low, urgent tone.

Hansen slid his blade back into place, looked at Wilkes and said, "It wouldn't be the first time."

CHAPTER THIRTEEN

Liz was at the hotel when Carla came by the next morning, and once again they had breakfast together. Over the coffee, Liz asked the Oriental girl to set up a meeting with Inspector Granger.

"Why do you want to meet with him?"

"Because we're both working on the same thing," Liz said. "We might as well work together."

"I don't know . . ."

"I don't know if he'll agree either, but the only way to find out is to ask. Will you do it?"

"Of course."

"Thanks, Carla."

"What are you going to do in the meantime?"

"I'm going to talk to Mr. Simonson, if I can find him. After that I'm going to have to talk to some of the people who knew Vincent Drake. From what his father said, that will include quite a few people in your business, Carla."

"Listen to me," Carla said, grabbing Liz's wrist across the table and gripping it tightly. "If you're going to question whores on the Barbary Coast and in Chinatown, you can't go alone."

"I'll be fine."

"You'll need a man with you, Liz, especially in Chinatown. Let me talk to my brother."

Liz was going to protest, but when she saw how worried Carla was, she decided to accept her offer.

"Oh, all right, Carla. Go ahead and talk to him — but not till you've talked to Granger."

"Good," Carla said, releasing Liz's wrist. "A woman can't go walking around Chinatown alone — especially not someone who looks like you."

Liz didn't bother telling Carla that she wasn't just any woman. She was Angel Eyes, and it was going to take all of her skills with a gun — and more — to clear herself of a murder charge.

When Carla left Liz she went to look for her brother before talking to Granger. She found Harry Lee in a Dupont Street gambling den.

"Little sister," he said as she sidled up next to him at a fan-tan table.

"I want to talk to you."

"So, talk."

"Alone."

Her brother looked at her, then smiled and said, "Come on."

He placed his hand against the small of her back and led her to a door at the rear of the room. He opened it without knocking and took her into an office.

"This place is owned by the tong?" she asked.

"Yes. I come by to . . . check on their interests."

"And to do some gambling."

He grinned and said, "Just a little."

Harry Lee was a handsome man, slender, not tall, but in good shape. He had a ready smile that women liked. His sister knew they liked it because some of her friends told her they did.

"I need a favor," Carla said.

"Name it."

She did. Harry listened intently, but before she had finished he was shaking his head.

"Little sister," he said. "You're asking me to get involved in a murder investigation."

"I'm asking you to help a friend of mine . . . and me."

He had his butt resting on top of the desk, his arms folded across his chest.

"Why do I let you talk me into things?"

"You never make me work hard at it, Harry," she said, leaning over to kiss him on the cheek.

"Granger is working on this, isn't he?"

"Yes."

"Has he asked you about me?"

"Yes."

"I'm going to end up talking to him if I hang around your friend, right?"

"I guess so."

He put his hands on her shoulders and kissed her on the forehead.

"The things I do for my little sister."

She hugged him and told him that he would find Liz at Zeke's later.

"That dump?"

"She needed a place to stay."

"Uh, Carla, your friend. She's not —?"

"No, she's not a whore."

"Is she pretty?"

She grinned and said, "You'll see."

She started for the door, and when she reached it she turned to look at her brother.

"Harry — "

"I know," he said, standing up. "Our parents didn't educate us so one of us would grow up to be a runner for the tong."

"I'll see you later," she said.

She knew why she loved her brother so much. All the times that she told him that their parents hadn't educated him to be a runner for the tong, he never once pointed out that they hadn't educated her so she could grow up to be a whore, either.

CHAPTER FOURTEEN

AGAIN LIZ ARCHER went to Kearny Street seeking Edward Simonson. This time he was in his office, with Thomas his nephew.

"Mr. Simonson?"

The elder Simonson looked up from his desk and frowned as she entered. Thomas, who had been leaning over his uncle's shoulder, stood up straight and smiled. Seeing both men side by side she could see where Thomas got his cleft chin.

Thomas spoke first. "This is the young lady I told you about last night, Uncle."

"I see." The elder Simonson stood up. He was a big, barrel-chested man in his sixties with a shock of snow-white hair and matching mutton-chop whiskers. "Is there something I can help you with, ma'am?" he said.

"Yes," said Liz. "My name is Elizabeth Archer, Mr. Simonson. I'd like to talk to you about Vincent Drake."

"The boy who was killed," Simonson said. "What a tragedy."

"Was it?"

"Of course," he replied. "It always is when someone is cut off in the prime of life."

"I see," said Liz non-committally. "Mr. Simonson, I understand that you didn't get along very well with Vincent Drake," she went on, although she knew the statement was not strictly true. She was just trying to get him to talk to her.

"That's not true," the man said. "As a matter of fact, my daughter was going to marry the boy."

"What about his father, Victor Drake?"

"Victor Drake and I are business rivals," Simonson admitted candidly. "However, that did not enter into the relationship between my daughter and his son."

"I see. Mr. Simonson — "

"Excuse me, young lady, but are you with the police?"

"I'm . . . working with the police to clear up a few questions."

"Such as?"

"Such as the relationships that existed between your family and the Drake family."

"The Drake family has always tried to undercut the Simonson family," young Thomas said.

"That's not strictly true," Simonson corrected his nephew, hardly bothering to look at the younger man while he did so. "The rivalry has all originated with Victor Drake. He and his children have never gotten along very well. Those are the relationships you should be checking into, Miss Archer."

"I intend to. I wonder, Mr. Simonson, if I'd be able to talk to your daughter."

"She's very distraught, but I'm sure she'd be willing to co-operate. You can find her at my ranch."

"I can take Miss Archer out there if you like, Uncle," Thomas Simonson offered.

The elder Simonson looked at his nephew now and nodded. "That might be a good idea, Tom," he said.

"I'll have to get my horse . . . " Liz began.

"That's all right," Thomas Simonson said eagerly. "I'll take you out there and bring you back in the buggy."

"That's very kind of you."

"Uncle, can we finish our business later?"

"Yes, of course." Simonson looked at Liz and said, "I hope you'll be understanding of my daughter's condition."

"I certainly will, sir."

"Shall we go?" Thomas Simonson asked, smiling so widely that his cleft chin looked like a bottomless pit.

Liz returned the smile. "Yes, let's," she answered.

As they approached the Simonson house in the buggy, Liz couldn't help but be impressed. Drake's house in town was large by city standards. But out here, several miles from San Francisco, there was room for a really impressive spread.

"This house looks like it belongs in the deep South," Liz said, marveling at the row of pillars that fronted the house.

"Uncle Edward is a southerner at heart. He saw a house like this in Louisiana and had it copied exactly — at great expense."

"It's beautiful."

"I guess," Thomas said, and guided the buggy through the front gate, which had been opened for them by a man armed with a shotgun.

"Why the guard?"

"Uncle insists on security. I think he's afraid someone might try to kill him."

"A business rival?"

"Or associate, even."

Could that have been why Simonson might have killed the younger Drake? Out of fear? Liz filed the possibility away in the back of her mind.

During the trip they had engaged in small talk about business and pleasure — with Thomas doing most of the talking — and Liz decided that Thomas, at eighteen or nineteen, was extremely sophisticated for his age. She couldn't help but wonder how experienced this lovely boy was with women.

Thomas directed the buggy to the front steps of the house, alighted and helped Liz down. He put his hands around her waist and set her on the ground gently, letting his hands linger on her waist a bit longer than necessary.

"Thank you."

"You're welcome."

"Shall we go in?"

Thomas motioned for Liz to precede him up the steps. When she reached the door she waited while he fitted a key into the lock and opened it.

The entry hall was huge. She knew there were two floors to the house from the rows of windows along the facade, but the foyer was two stories high and soared upward to a cathedral ceiling.

"Uncle loves this hall."

"I can understand why."

"I can't."

He started to walk ahead of her, but Liz put her hand on his arm to stop him.

"Thomas, I get the impression you don't like this house."

"That's not an impression, that's a fact."

"Why?"

He spread his arms in a gesture that encompassed his surroundings and said, "There's no life in this house. No life and no love."

He was about to go on when someone called his name from the second floor.

"Thomas?"

Liz looked up to see a woman approach the staircase and descend to meet them. To say she wasn't pretty was being kind, and Liz could see why Simonson might have tried to marry her off to Vincent Drake. No man would want her unless a piece of the family business came with her. That was cruel, Liz knew, but this woman was . . . plain. There was no other word for it. It was obvious why Vincent Drake had not been interested in her.

Actually, her figure was not that bad. Her breasts were firm although her body was rather angular, as was her face. Her jaw was too long, and she had the Simonson cleft chin in an exaggerated form, as if her chin were made of two separate bones. Her lips were thin, and sharp cheekbones gave her face a gaunt, hollow look.

Plain might have been a kind word, as well.

"Hello, Gabby," Thomas said. He approached his cousin and kissed her cheek affectionately. He didn't care about her appearance. She was his cousin, and he loved her.

"Darling," she replied, and turned her head to kiss him on the mouth. Liz shivered as Gabrielle's narrow lips touched those of her beautiful male cousin. Was there something more than family affection in Gabrielle's eyes?

Liz put the woman's age at roughly twenty-eight or so, almost ten years more than her cousin.

"And who is this?" Gabrielle asked.

"This is Elizabeth Archer, Gabby," Thomas said. "She's a friend of mine."

"How nice," Gabrielle said coldly, and Liz shivered again. The look in the woman's eyes was almost malevolent.

"She wants to talk to you, Gabby."

"About what?"

"About Vincent."

"Really?" the woman said, looking at her cousin and then turning a bored look Liz's way. "Were you one of his whores, honey?"

"Gabby!"

"I'm just asking, darling," Gabrielle said, feigning innocence.

"Elizabeth is not a whore."

"What is she, then?"

"She's working with the police to find out who killed Vincent."

"Really?" Gabrielle said again, her tone disbelieving.

The woman did not look to Liz like someone who was distraught over the death of a man she had loved.

"I'd like to ask you a few questions."

"Well, then, why don't we get comfortable? Let's go into the study. Darling," she said to Thomas, "be a dear and get us some tea." She cupped his chin in her hand and kissed him on the mouth again.

Thomas threw Liz an embarrassed look and said, "Excuse me."

As Thomas went to the kitchen, Gabrielle said, "Let's go this way, Elizabeth."

Liz walked next to Gabrielle, noticing that the woman was a few inches taller than she was, almost as tall as Thomas.

"He's a dear boy, isn't he?" Gabrielle said.

"He's very nice."

"And beautiful, don't you think?"

"He's . . . attractive."

"Oh, he's more than that," Gabrielle said, giving Liz a sideways look. "Just between us girls . . . he has an absolutely beautiful body. Have you seen him naked?"

"I have not."

"I have," Gabrielle said with great satisfaction.

"Could we talk about Vincent?"

"He's not very experienced in bed," Gabrielle said, "but I'm working on him."

Liz closed her eyes. Unbidden, the spectacle of Thomas Simonson naked in bed with his cousin sprang to mind. She shook her head slightly to dispel it.

"Does that shock you?"

"Is that why you said it?" Liz asked her. "To try to shock me?"

"No," Gabrielle said. "Just letting you know, Elizabeth, that Thomas and I are very . . . close."

They reached the study and Gabrielle waved Liz toward a seat.

"Does incest disgust you?" Gabrielle asked, sitting across from her.

"I've never thought about it."

"Well, it doesn't disgust us," she said. "In fact, it runs in the Simonson family."

"What runs in the family?" Thomas Simonson asked, entering the room.

Gabrielle looked up quickly and said, "The chin, darling,

the chin.'' Then she looked at Liz as if daring her to call her a liar. Liz kept silent.

"Consuelo will bring the tea.''

"I really don't have time for tea, Thomas,'' Liz said, standing up. She couldn't bear to be in the same room with the other woman any longer.

"Oh, really?'' Gabrielle said, standing up. "Do you have to leave so soon?''

"I just remembered an appointment. Thomas, would you take me back to town?''

"I had hoped you'd stay with me a while, Thomas,'' Gabrielle said.

"I have to take Elizabeth back to town, Gabby. I'll be out later.''

"All right, darling.'' Gabrielle kissed Thomas again and glared at Liz, holding her cousin's arm possessively.

Liz turned and started for the front door, and Thomas had to hurry to catch up. Outside he helped her into the buggy and climbed up next to her.

"I thought you wanted to talk to her about the murder?''

"That's all right, Thomas,'' Liz said. "I found out what I wanted to know.''

There was no doubt in her mind that Gabrielle Simonson was capable — very capable — of murder.

CHAPTER FIFTEEN

THEY RODE BACK to San Francisco in a silence that was largely enforced by Liz. When they had returned the buggy, Thomas once again asked Liz if they could get to know one another better.

"I'm a little occupied at the moment, Thomas," she said, "but I know where to find you."

"Let me give you my address."

"You don't live — ?"

"In that house? Hell, no." He told Liz his address, and she promised that she would get in touch with him as soon as she got "this matter cleared up."

If the truth were told, she would have liked very much to have dinner with him — and whatever came after — but she couldn't dispel the vision of him and Gabrielle in bed together, and it sickened her. It made her angry, as well, because the woman could have been lying, maliciously, but until Liz could shake that feeling, she knew she and

Thomas would never have a chance to get to know each other better.

And she regretted it.

Carla Lee closed her eyes and allowed herself to drift while Dan Granger worked busily between her legs. His educated tongue was taking her to higher planes than she'd ever achieved before, even with him. He was the only man who could make her come. Maybe that was the only reason she loved him, but she didn't think so. There was more to it than that.

In any case, the man really knew how to pay a debt, she couldn't deny it.

She cupped the back of his head, pressing his face deeper into her pussy. He inhaled the sweet odor of her musk and flicked his tongue around her clit. She came immediately, grinding her butt into the sheet as he continued to lick her, even after her tremors had faded, until she was so sensitive that she begged him to stop . . .

Afterward she said, "Liz Archer wants to meet with you, Dan."

"When?"

"Tonight, I guess."

"Why?"

"She figures you're both working on the same case so you might as well work together."

"That's kind of her," Granger said wryly. "I guess she figures I can use all the help I can get."

"No, I think she realizes that it's the other way around."

Granger thought it over for a moment and then said, "All right, bring her here."

"To your place?" Carla asked, surprised.

He cupped her right breast and circled the nipple with his tongue.

"If I'll let you come here," he teased, "I'll let anybody."

"You bastard!" she said. She pushed him onto his back, slithered down so that her face was between his legs and started to lick his balls. She was going to use every ounce of experience she had to make him beg her to let him come in her mouth.

This was the only time she ever knew that he wanted her, when they were in bed together, and she was going to make the most of it.

Joe Dunn stood in a doorway across from Zeke's hotel, which Liz Archer had just entered.

Dunn had followed Liz to Edward Simonson's office, to Simonson's ranch, and back again without being seen. That was just part of his job, but he was good at tailing and proud of it. He knew that at best he was a nondescript-looking character, which was the reason Granger used him for these kinds of jobs.

He had followed her back to her hotel, left his horse tied down the street and taken up his position in the doorway across the street.

He had no way of knowing that Harry Lee was inside waiting for her.

Liz had no way of knowing either, so when she entered her room and saw the Oriental man seated on the bed she prepared to draw her gun if necessary.

"Easy, lady," the man said, holding his hands out to show her they were empty.

"How'd you get in here?"

"Zeke let me in."

"Why?"

"I'm Harry Lee."

"Carla's brother?"

"That's right."

Liz relaxed. Seeing that, so did Harry Lee.

"I thought you were going to blow my head off there for a minute."

"I was prepared to."

"I'll bet you were."

"You and Carla speak real good English," Liz commented. She had wanted to ask Carla about that.

"Our parents saw to that — got us some schooling," he said. "How would you like me to speak, like a laundry boy?"

"You're doing fine."

"My little sister says you need looking after."

"No," Liz said, moving toward the only chair in the room and sitting on it. "But I do need a guide through Chinatown — and maybe the Barbary Coast."

"What are you looking for?"

"Somebody who'd want to kill Vincent Drake."

"You'd have an easier time if you looked for people who wanted to kill his father."

"His father is still alive," Liz pointed out. "I'm more interested in who *did* kill Vincent."

He shrugged and said, "I am here to serve."

He stood up and she saw that he was just a few inches taller than she was — about as tall as Gabrielle Simonson. She wished she could stop thinking about that woman and what she had said about her cousin Thomas.

She wished she could stop thinking about Thomas Simonson, too; rarely had she seen a man that she would call beautiful, but Tom certainly fit that description.

Critically, she examined Harry Lee. He was very slim, but he moved with great confidence and grace. He was attractive, although she had never been attracted to a Chinese man before — in fact, she had never known any.

"Are we leaving now?" he asked.

"I think we should wait for Carla."

"What should we do in the meantime?"

"Maybe we should get to know each other better."

He stared at her with his eyes narrowed and said, "Does that mean what I think it means?"

"I've had a very unpleasant experience, today," she said, standing up abruptly. "One that I'd like to forget." She began to unbutton her shirt and said, "I'm asking you to help me forget."

Her decision had been a spur-of-the-moment one, but she felt that she needed this for several reasons.

She finished unbuttoning her shirt and dropped it to the floor. Harry Lee caught his breath when he saw her breasts. They were large, rounded and firm, with pink nipples and wide aureoles. He had never seen such beautiful breasts before, even on the classiest whores — and he had run through most of San Francisco's girls for hire.

Liz unbuckled her gunbelt and hung it on the back of the chair, then sat down and began to pull her boots off. She stopped when she saw that he wasn't moving and stared at him. "Well?" she said.

In a flurry of motion he discarded his clothing and his boots and stood there naked as Liz slid her pants down over her hips to her ankles and kicked them away. One more wisp of cloth and she was naked.

He *was* thin, but he wasn't skinny. His upper torso was

hard, with not an ounce of fat, and there were ridges on his stomach. His penis was fully erect. She saw that it was not very large.

Still, she was sure he would manage to keep her mind off unpleasant things . . . for a while.

He studied her, and she stood there, almost posing for him, hands on hips, breasts thrust forward, legs a little apart. She could see that he was staring at the triangle of golden hair between her thighs. In turn she stared at the wiry black growth from which his penis jutted, and he smiled and reached for her.

She approached him and pressed her full breasts against his chest. He encircled her with his strong arms, and they kissed, tentatively at first, and then with more urgency. She concentrated on the way his lips felt on hers, the way his tongue entered her mouth, the way his hands roved over her body, squeezing, rubbing, sliding between her legs and arousing her.

He bent his head to kiss her breasts, then continued to work his way down her body. Dropping to his knees he kissed her belly, laved her naval with his tongue, and then probed through her blonde pubic patch, enjoying the taste of her excitement.

She cupped his head in her hands, leaning her hips into the pressure of his tongue and mouth, but she was having trouble letting herself go. Sensing that she wasn't going to be able to achieve orgasm she urged him back to his feet, so they could try it on the bed.

They moved to the bed and fell on it together, with him on top. He began to run his mouth over her breasts, biting her nipples while sliding a finger between her legs. Finding her wet and ready, he slid first one finger inside of her and then another. He withdrew his fingers, licked her wetness off, and then put them back in. Under other circumstances she might have found that excitingly erotic.

"I want you inside of me," she said, in his ear. "All the way inside."

Eager to please, he withdrew his fingers, mounted her, probed her moist portal with the head of his small cock, and then rammed it home. It *was* small, she thought, but he knew how to use it. He slid his hands beneath her, cupped her buttocks to draw her up to him and began to drive himself into her. His body was hard, his hands strong as he squeezed her ass, and his cock, in spite of its size — or lack of it — was finding places inside of her that Victor Drake's bigger organ had not been able to touch.

She wrapped her legs around his hips, encircled his body with her arms and went with his tempo until suddenly he erupted inside her. She had thought she'd be able to achieve completion with him, but her mind was still partially elsewhere and she was unable to. She simply moaned as if she had achieved orgasm, the way she used to when she was pretending to be a whore in Diablo City, Texas.

Pretending? She *had* done everything a whore would do and, although it was in a good cause, she was a little uncomfortable about how easily she seemed to be able to fit back into the "disguise."

"Sorry," he said, sliding off her.

"For what?"

He gave her a look and said, "I've been with enough women — and with enough whores — to know when a woman is faking it, Elizabeth."

"Then I'm sorry," she said, running her hand over his taut, flat stomach. "You did everything right, Harry. It's just me."

"Maybe we can try again some other time."

"No maybe about it, Harry," she assured him. "We will. But right now we'd better get dressed so we'll be ready when your sister gets here."

As they dressed, Harry asked, "And what do we do while we're waiting . . . this time?"

She shrugged and said, "You got a deck of cards?"

He grinned. "It just so happens I do."

Liz decided she liked Harry Lee . . . a lot.

When Carla arrived she studied her brother and Liz thoughtfully for a few moments. They were playing poker, but she got the impression something else might have gone on earlier.

"You two get acquainted?" she asked.

"We did," Harry said.

Carla looked at Liz and said, "Granger says he'll see you later tonight."

"Where?"

"At his home."

"What's the address?"

"Harry knows where it is. After dark, he'll take you there."

Liz looked at Harry and said, "That gives us some time to go to Chinatown."

"If that's what you want, Liz." Harry looked at his sister and said, "Carla?"

"She's not coming," Liz said, before Carla could answer. "She's done enough."

"I have to make a living, anyway," Carla said. She pinned her brother with a hard stare and said, "You better watch out for her, Harry."

"I have the feeling, little sister," Harry said, eyeing Liz and the gun on her hip, "that it could also work the other way around.

CHAPTER SIXTEEN

DUPONT STREET and Ross Alley were typical of Chinatown, catering to gamblers and to men—and women—in search of "expert" companionship. Also available were Chinatown's numerous opium dens, for those who simply wanted to lose themselves in a drug-induced haze and forget their troubles.

"Harry, how do you know which places Vincent Drake frequented?" Liz asked as Harry led her through the dark streets and alleys of his home turf.

"They'd be the same places everyone goes to, Liz — everyone, that is, who can afford them and knows where to find them."

"Meaning?"

"Meaning that people like the Drakes and Simonsons of San Francisco don't frequent the same places that a sailor off a ship would."

"Did you know Drake?"

"I've seen him," Harry said. "Those people and my people don't exactly travel in the same circles, either. Let's go in here."

He took her into a fan-tan parlor, but did not let her ask any questions.

"Let's just listen for a while," he suggested. "The murder is recent enough that we might hear something."

They stopped in a few places just to listen, with Liz keeping her hair under her hat as a result of Harry's suggestion.

"Not that it will help," he said. "You obviously have too much class for Chinatown."

"Not necessarily."

"You can't help the way you look, Liz," he replied. "You belong in a gown in Portsmouth Square."

"I'd be too uncomfortable."

After they'd hit a few gambling establishments Liz asked, "What about drugs?"

"What about them?"

"Was Drake interested?"

"I'd have to ask around."

"Why can't we — ?"

"I don't want to take you to any places like that," Harry interrupted her.

"Why not?"

"For one thing, you're a lady," he said. "For another thing, you're white. And for a third thing, you're beautiful — "

"And all of that means . . . ?"

"All of that means that no one will believe that you're there just to smoke an opium pipe. I'll have to go alone, smoke a little, talk a little and see what I can find out."

"Won't that be dangerous for you?"

He grinned and said, "No. It will be just another day, for me."

He looked at the sky and added, "It's almost dark. I'd better take you to Granger's."

"Do you know Granger?"

"Sure. He's always trying to get me to travel the path of the law-abiding."

"You don't, normally?"

"Uh, let's just say that I've been known to straddle it from time to time."

"What about Carla?"

"What about her?"

"What's her relationship with Granger? Is she in love with him?"

"Have you seen them together?"

"No."

"Then how could you know that?"

Liz shrugged and said, "I've heard her talk about him, and I know she does him favors . . ."

"Yeah, she's in love with him," Harry said. "And she's just going to end up getting hurt."

"Why?"

"He doesn't care for her," Harry Lee said, and Liz could tell from the tone of his voice and the look on his face that he really loved his sister.

"Harry, forgive me for saying this, but Carla seems too smart to have to be a — "

"Whore? I agree, but then I'm too smart to be what I am. We are what we are, Liz, just like you are what you are — whatever that is."

Liz didn't want to get into that. She didn't know if Inspector Granger knew she was Angel Eyes. If he did, he was probably sorry he'd let her out of jail. The fact that he hadn't pulled her in again puzzled her.

Why not? she wondered.

The answer to that would have to wait until she could talk to him.

"All right," she said. "Let's go and see Inspector Granger."

Harry Lee took Liz to Granger's residential hotel on Market Street and stopped outside.

"You're not coming up?" Liz asked.

"No," he said, shaking his head. "The inspector and I don't see eye to eye on a few things. You go ahead. I'll meet you at your hotel . . . in the morning."

"All right, Harry. Thanks for your help."

"Sure, Liz," he said.

After Liz Archer entered the hotel, Harry Lee stood there for a few moments, deep in thought, then shrugged and began to make his way back to Chinatown.

Now he'd be able to get some real work done.

Liz asked the clerk on duty where she could find Inspector Granger. The man, who had been alerted to expect her arrival, told her that the inspector's suite was on the second floor and gave her the number.

She went upstairs, feeling some nervousness. Would Granger be waiting for her with a couple of uniformed policemen, ready to take her back to jail? Somehow, she didn't think so. Even if he wanted to take her back he'd do it himself.

She knocked on his door and waited to see if she was right.

Granger opened the door and smiled at her.

"Come in, Angel Eyes."

CHAPTER SEVENTEEN

"COME IN," he said again.

She entered slowly. Now that she realized he knew who she was, she was puzzled.

"You're wondering how I know who you are?" he asked, closing the door behind them.

"You didn't know originally?"

"No, I didn't," he admitted.

The room they were in was a sitting room, and he invited her to take a seat. The room was furnished with a sofa, an armchair and, in one corner, a desk. Some newspapers were spread out on one end of the sofa, and on the desk was a stack of files.

"Can I get you something to drink?"

"Why don't we just talk?" Liz suggested.

"All right."

Granger picked the newspapers up off the sofa and deposited them on the floor. Liz sat on the sofa and he sat in the armchair.

"I understand you think I need help on this case," Granger said. "My chief thinks I had the killer and let her go."

"He knows you let me out?"

He didn't bother denying it to her.

"Slip through my fingers, let's say," he amended.

"Well, I don't think you need the help, Inspector," she said. "I think I do. Your help."

"That's why you're here? To ask for my help?"

"Next to me, you're the expert on this matter. Also, you know a lot more than I do about this town and the people involved."

"That's true."

"And you don't think I did it."

"That's true, too."

"Why not?"

"You had no motive," he said. "And you're not a whore. Vincent tended to stick to prostitutes. Also, we found a dead Chinese whore — knifed — that same night, floating in the bay."

"You think she's connected with Drake's death?"

"It's possible," he said. "Why don't you tell me what you've found out from Victor Drake and the Simonsons?"

"The man you have following me must be very good," she said. "I never saw him."

"That's why I use him." Granger stood up, walked to his window, which overlooked the main street, and peered out. "He's across the street right now."

"I'm glad for his sake that it's a mild night."

Granger returned to the armchair and stared at her.

Liz started talking, telling him about her conversations with Victor Drake and the Simonson family.

"They're quite a bunch, aren't they?" Granger asked. "The Simonsons, I mean."

"Oh yes, that they are."

"Edward's got the power, Thomas has the youth and looks, and Gabrielle — well, she's got all the bitterness."

"I can't argue with that."

"And any one of them would be capable of having killed Vincent Drake."

She frowned and said, "Thomas, too?"

"Especially Thomas," he said. "His mother left Thomas's father — also named Thomas — for Drake."

"Then Thomas, Junior, and Vincent Drake were brothers?"

"No," Granger said. "Mrs. Simonson and Drake never got married. She died first. Drake's own children were already born — and their mother had died — when Drake and Thomas's mother had their little fling."

"And Thomas blames Victor Drake for mistreating his mother?"

"Edward Simonson does, and he's instilled that in Thomas ever since he was very young."

"Thomas seems . . . decent, and nice."

"Oh, he is, but he does what the old man tells him to do. For that matter, he does whatever Gabrielle tells him to do, as well. He hasn't got much of a mind of his own."

"I see."

"Where else have you been?"

"Well, you know that."

"I haven't had a chance to get a message from my man yet about this evening," Granger explained. "I could walk across the street, but why don't you tell me?"

"Chinatown."

"Chinatown?" He frowned. "You went to Chinatown alone?"

"No, not alone."

"Oh, I see," the inspector said, as understanding dawned on him. "Harry Lee."

"He's been very helpful."

"Well, maybe it will keep him out of trouble," Granger said. "I hope so."

"You care about him?"

"Sure. He's basically a nice kid."

"And his sister?"

"She's a good kid, too."

"No, I mean do you like her, too?"

"Sure."

"She's in love with you, you know."

"Is that what you came here to discuss?"

"No, it isn't," she said. "What are you doing to prove that I'm innocent?"

"Nothing."

"What?"

Granger frowned and said, "I'm not your defense lawyer, Elizabeth. May I call you Elizabeth?"

"Liz."

"Liz. It's your job to prove that you didn't kill Vincent Drake. It's only my job to try and find out who did. If it turns out to be you, then that's it."

"I see."

"However, there's still no reason that we can't work together on this."

"How do you propose we do that?"

"Easy. You tell me everything that you find out."

"And you tell me what you find out?"

He wavered on that.

"Well . . . "

"I see," Liz said. "I work with you, but you don't work with me."

Granger stroked his jaw and said. "That's my offer."

Liz shook her head and said, "You must have a lot of friends, Inspector."

"I don't need friends, Liz," he said. "And you can call me Dan."

"If I did would that make us friends?"

"Not necessarily."

"And what about Carla and her brother? Are they your friends?"

"Why bring them into this?"

"I'm just trying to figure out where I stand," Liz said. "I like Harry and Carla, but he is what I guess you would call a law-breaker, and she is a prostitute. You know that I'm called 'Angel Eyes' in some parts of the country. Does that put me in a class with them in your view?"

"There are only two classes of people in my book, Liz," Granger said. "First there's me, and then there's everyone else. That's the way I think."

"You must be a lonely man."

"I get by."

"No, that's not what I meant. I'm sure you have your share of bed partners, Inspector, but that doesn't mean that you aren't lonely."

She stood up, preparing to leave.

"I'll keep my man following you . . . just in case," Granger said.

"Just in case I get into trouble?"

He walked her to the door, opened it for her and smiled.

"Just in case you try to leave town."

As she stepped outside the hotel, Liz spotted Granger's man across the street. He realized that she had seen him, but he didn't bother to look away. She crossed the street and approached him.

"What's your name?" she asked.

"Dunn," he replied. "Joe Dunn."

"Well, stay close, Mr. Dunn. The inspector seems to think I may try to leave town."

"I'm sure the inspector didn't say that exactly, ma'am," Dunn said. It was dark, but she could see that there was nothing remarkable about Joe Dunn's looks. No wonder she hadn't seen him before. He simply blended in with the background.

"No," she said. "No, you're right. He didn't say that, exactly. All right, I'm going back to my hotel now."

"Yes, ma'am."

"If you'd like to get something to eat — ?"

"That's all right, ma'am," he said. "I'm not that hungry."

"What if I paid for it?"

"I'm sorry, ma'am," Dunn said in a neutral tone. "I couldn't do that."

"I'm sorry," Liz said awkwardly. "I didn't mean to try and compromise you."

"I know you didn't."

She stood there for a few moments, exchanging glances with the man in the doorway. He looked at her as if she were a lamppost or something equally inanimate. Again, she thought she knew why Granger had decided to use this particular man for this job.

"Thank you, Mr. Dunn."

"That's all right, Miss Archer."

"Well, good night," she said, and started down the street, with him following behind her. It dawned on her that since they were going to the same place they could have walked together, but Dunn — good policeman that he was — would probably have rejected that idea, as well.

She wasn't even sure why she had crossed the street to talk to him. Maybe she just wanted to make sure that the man who was following her was competent.

Since that seemed to be the case, she was satisfied.

Joe Dunn could not be faulted for failing to see the man who watched from a darkened doorway further down the street. After all, Joe's job was to follow and keep an eye on Liz Archer, and this man had been in position well before either Dunn or Liz arrived.

Wilkes saw Liz Archer walk away, after briefly conversing with a man across the street from the hotel. He'd positioned himself across and down the street from Granger's hotel hoping that she would show up, but now he realized he'd gotten more than he'd bargained for.

The woman seemed to have a policeman watching her pretty constantly, and that was going to make getting to her just that much more difficult. Of course, Wilkes's employer would not take that news gracefully, so Wilkes had no intention of telling him.

He left his doorway and started out after them. As soon as he found out where the girl was staying he would meet up with Hansen and make plans for getting rid of her.

First, though, they'd have to make plans to get rid of the policeman. Wilkes was against killing lawmen — especially a lawman like Granger, because that would bring Steelman looking for his killers. The police chief had a lot of regard for the inspector and wouldn't take kindly to having his fair-haired boy killed.

This lawman wasn't Granger, though. He was just someone assigned to follow the girl — either to look after her, or to make sure she didn't leave town. Whichever it was, that meant there was still a very active investigation going on, and killing the girl was the only way to stop it.

But first, the lawman.

CHAPTER EIGHTEEN

THE FOLLOWING MORNING Harry Lee showed up early, just before daybreak, and knocked on Liz's door.

"Who is it?" she called out.

"Harry Lee."

Since he wasn't exactly a stranger, Liz decided to answer the door straight from bed, clad only in her underthings.

"That's not a healthy sight for a man who's been up all night," he said, sidling past her into the room without taking his eyes off her.

"What have you been doing up all night?" she asked, closing the door.

"Working for you," he said, sitting on her bed. It was still warm from her, and he decided to lie back on it.

"Do you want to explain that?"

"Do you want to lie down here beside me?" he asked. "I can't lift my head to look at you."

"That's flattering," she said, but she climbed back in bed next to him.

"I prowled the notorious opium dens of Chinatown last night," he explained. "At first I just listened. Then, after a while, I started asking questions about Vincent Drake."

"Wasn't that dangerous?"

"It would have been, for you," he replied. "Not for me."

"All right," she said. "I accept that. What did you find out?"

"Are you ready?"

"I'm ready."

His eyes had been closed up to this point, but now he opened them and looked at her lying next to him, propped up on one elbow. She looked so beautiful, her face still a bit swollen from sleep, her hair tousled, her breasts partially visible, that he wished he had more to tell her.

"Nothing."

She stared at him. "Nothing? You mean, nothing at all?"

"I mean nothing at all," he repeated. "Apparently, Drake had been to some of the opium dens, but he wasn't a regular customer. The feeling I got was that he tried it a few times and didn't like it. He didn't go to any of them long enough to make enemies."

"So what we've got," Liz said, "is the Simonsons and possibly enemies made from gambling."

"We can probably clear up the gambling part today," he said, rubbing his eyes. "In Chinatown, at least. After that we can check Portsmouth Square and the Barbary Coast."

"Victor Drake said that Portsmouth Square was not a favorite haunt of his son's."

"No, apparently he preferred to go slumming," Harry

said. "We should probably check all of the whorehouses in Chinatown, while we're at it. He might have made some enemies there."

"Good idea," Liz said.

"I have another good idea," Harry said, with his eyes closed.

"What?"

"Sleep."

"But I have a better idea," Liz countered.

"What?" Harry asked.

She snaked her hand inside his shirt and rubbed his hairless chest. Her hand was warm. As she snuggled up closer to him, Harry became aware that her entire body was still warm from a night in bed. He began to respond, and she noticed.

"I see you like my idea better than yours," she said, moving her hand from his chest to his swollen crotch.

"I haven't the strength to undress," he said wearily.

"I'll take care of that."

He opened his eyes a crack so he could watch her. First she divested herself of her "bed clothes," and he watched in fascination as her full breasts bounced and swayed while she undressed him.

Truly, she had the better idea.

Liz removed Harry Lee's boots first, then unbuckled his pants and slid them off. The bulge in his shorts was throbbing, and she caressed it gently, trailing her fingertips lightly over his swollen balls. He moaned, moving his hips slightly. She looked at him but his eyes still appeared to be closed.

Liz was surprised to find that she was becoming excited. Surprised — and grateful. She guessed she was finally throwing off the effects of her meeting with Gabrielle Simonson. The woman's actions no longer inhibited her own attitudes toward sex, and she found that she very much wanted to have sex with this handsome man.

She removed his shorts and dropped them on the floor. His penis, slender and hard, prodded at the air. His legs were as hairless as his chest, but he was hard muscle all over. She ran her hands over the smooth flesh of his thighs, enjoying the feel of his taut muscles. She leaned over him and allowed his penis to creep between her full breasts. Squeezing her breasts together she began to pull gently on his rigid organ, rolling it gently between her breasts. His stiff cock was hot and getting hotter by the moment.

As was she.

Releasing his cock she began to run her tongue and lips over his thighs. He spread his legs to allow her easy access to his inner thighs.

She shifted around so that she was between his spread legs and looked at his face. He appeared to be asleep, but she knew he was feigning. He was still wearing his shirt, but she would get to that later.

She leaned over and poked at his balls with her nose, flicking her tongue out to lick them gently. Again he moaned and lifted his hips. She ran her tongue up the underside of his penis, circled the swollen, mushroom-like head, and licked down the other side while caressing his balls with her hand. He continued to fake sleeping until she finally opened her mouth and allowed his hard, slim penis to enter her mouth. She began to suck it lovingly.

He no longer pretended to be asleep.

He reached down to cup her head while she continued to suck on his cock. She worked her way down to the root, and then back up again, alternately taking his entire penis into her mouth, and then almost releasing it, retaining only the swollen head.

When she felt his penis and balls begin to swell in prelude to coming, she allowed him to slip from her mouth completely. She reached up and began to unbutton his shirt. With his help, she removed the remainder of his clothes. He was now totally naked — and very much awake.

She moved up so that she was sitting across his hips with his penis pinned beneath her. She slid her soaking pussy up and down the length of his cock, placing the palms of her hands on his chest. He reached for her, grasped her hips, lifted her up with surprising — or not so surprising — strength and impaled her on his cock.

She began to rotate her hips, driving herself down on his hardness, and she leaned over him so that he could reach her breasts. His lips and tongue drew her nipples taut while he plumbed her depths, driving her toward a very real and long-overdue orgasm. When he began to spurt inside of her she opened her mouth and cried out happily as her own orgasm overtook her, allowing her to join him in completion. He groaned and raised his hips, biting her nipple so hard that he caused a jolt of exquisite pain to shoot through her.

She slid off after he had softened inside of her and kissed him gently on the mouth.

"Now," she said, "you can go to sleep."

"What about you?"

"Oh, I'll take a little nap," she said, stretching her naked body luxuriously. "But I'll have to go out soon."

"Don't go out alone," he said, sleepily. "Wake me up."

"Okay."

"Liz?"

"Hmm?" she replied, sounding as sleepy as he did.

"Guess this time was a little better, huh?"

"This time," she said, laying her hand over his crotch and lovingly caressing his limp organ, "was a *lot* better!"

Liz was leaning over a basin of water washing the sleep from her eyes when Harry Lee woke up.

"Hey!" he called.

She turned, water rolling down her face and her full, naked breasts.

"You didn't wake me."

"I figured I'd let you sleep a little longer," she told him, reaching for a towel. She dried her face and her breasts, careful of the right one because the nipple was still tender. Harry Lee had sharp teeth.

"Are you leaving?"

"I have some things to do this morning, Harry," she said, reaching for her shirt. "I don't really need you. Stay asleep."

"What things?"

"I've got to see a man."

"Who?"

"Thomas Simonson."

"The pretty boy," Harry Lee said, scowling. It was obvious he didn't think much of Simonson.

"He might be able to tell me who killed Vincent Drake, Harry," she said, buttoning her shirt. "Especially if it was one of his own family."

"And if it was, why would he tell you?"

"I get the impression he doesn't like his family too much," she said, reaching for her gunbelt now. Buckling it around her hips she added, "He might grab at the chance to break away from them."

"A man should love his family," Harry said.

"I know you love Carla and she loves you," Liz replied. "Do you have any other family?"

He shook his head.

"Our parents were killed when we were young. They were stoned to death by a bunch of Shasta County miners who figured it was better to blame some Chinese for the fact that they couldn't find any gold than to blame themselves."

"That's awful."

"Look," he said, changing the subject. "Just promise me you won't go anywhere near Chinatown and the Barbary Coast without me."

"I promise. I've also got to go and see Drake's brother and sister. Do you know anything about them?"

"No."

"Apparently their father isn't too happy with any of them. I'm curious to find out why."

She started for the door and he said to her, "Just watch your step."

"I always watch my step, Harry," she said, opening the door. "I'll be back here later to wake you up."

He didn't hear her. Harry Lee had already fallen back to sleep. She closed the door gently behind her when she left so as not to wake him.

CHAPTER NINETEEN

LIZ KNEW all along that she would have to use sex on Thomas Simonson to get what she wanted. For one thing, he was a young man and she was an older — though not that much older — and very beautiful woman. Young men often fantasized about older women, and she knew that young men would do a lot to make their fantasies come true.

Second, if he was indeed engaging in incestuous sex with his ugly cousin, he would probably jump at the chance to make love with someone who looked like Liz Archer — which would probably ruin him for his cousin for life.

That idea appealed to her, greatly.

Since he had given her his address she did not think he'd mind having her drop in on him before nine o'clock. Of course, he might already have left for one of his uncle's warehouses, but she decided to take that chance.

Tom Simonson lived in a residential hotel very much like the one Inspector Granger lived in, but on Diamond

Street. She had no doubt that Simonson paid for his. As far as Granger was concerned, she had an open mind.

"I would like to see Mr. Simonson," she said to the clerk, who was gaping at her. "Has he left, yet?"

"Uh, no, he hasn't."

"What suite is he in?"

The clerk replied automatically, before it dawned on him that it might not have been wise to.

"Sixteen."

"Thank you."

"Uh, ma'am — " he called out, but Liz ignored him and hurried up the steps. She found suite sixteen and knocked loudly.

"Coming," Thomas Simonson's voice called out. "Who is it?"

"Liz Archer."

Hurried footsteps approached the door from the other side and then it swung open to reveal Tom Simonson. He had obviously been in the act of dressing, and his shirt had yet to be buttoned. His chest was very hairy, unlike Harry Lee's, and broad.

"Liz!"

"May I come in?"

"Of course."

As she entered she could smell coffee and suddenly had an urge for some.

"Have I interrupted your breakfast?"

"No," he said, closing the door, "I've finished. I have some coffee left, if you like."

"That would be very nice."

There was a tray on a table in a corner and he went to it, poured some coffee into a cup and handed it to her.

"I hope you don't mind using my cup," he said. "I wasn't expecting company."

"How old are you, Tom?" she asked.

"Twenty."

He was older than Liz had thought, but still a few years younger than she.

"Why?" he asked.

"Just curious."

"Do you think I'm too young for you?" he asked. "Is that it? Or too inexperienced?"

"Experience doesn't matter," she said, sipping her coffee. "You could be inexperienced now, but if we went to bed, you'd soon be experienced."

"Well, I'm not."

"Not what?"

"Inexperienced."

"Oh," she said. "Then I guess you wouldn't be interested in going to bed with me."

He gaped at her for a moment. "By God!" he said, and reached for her.

"After my coffee," she said, backing away a little.

His eyes narrowed then and his face took on a look she hadn't seen before. Before she could interpret it, it was gone.

"You're joking with me."

"About going to bed with you?" she asked. She moved closer to him, holding the coffee cup in one hand, and toyed with the hair on his chest with the other. "You're a very good-looking young man, Thomas. Did you know that?"

"Yes."

"Oh, and you're modest, too," she said, laughing.

"Do you know that you're beautiful?"

"Yes."

"Then I'm as modest as you are."

He reached for her again, and she put the coffee cup down as he encircled her in his powerful arms. She pressed her hands against his chest as he kissed her, clumsily at first. He was overeager, and so she used her mouth and hands subtly to "teach" him without seeming to.

"That was very nice," she said. Against her thigh she could feel his huge erection. In spite of herself — and her early morning session with Harry Lee — her interest was aroused.

"Why did you come here this morning?" he asked, holding her fast in his arms. She became aware of how truly strong he was when she tried to move away and couldn't.

"You're very strong."

"Why?"

"I came because I'm attracted to you."

"Really? Didn't you come here to ask me questions?"

"Yes," she said, deciding that to be honest was her best course — at least, in part. "I'm also frightened for you."

"Why?"

"I don't like your cousin."

"Gabby?"

"Yes. I think she's a horrible woman."

"She can't help the way she looks — "

"It's more than that," Liz broke in. She tried to back away again but he held her fast. "The things she said . . ."

"Like what?"

"Thomas," Liz said. "I don't want to talk about it . . ."

She pressed her face against his chest, playing for time. He smelled good: masculine and fresh. She kissed his chest, twirling her tongue around one of his nipples.

"Liz — "

"Yes?" she said. She pushed her hands beneath his shirt, then slid it off him, dropping it to the floor. She began to cover his broad chest with kisses, licking his nipples, biting them . . .

"Jesus!" he said hoarsely.

He loosened his hold on her then and reached for the buttons on her shirt.

"I'll do it," she said. "You get undressed. I want you, Tom Simonson."

She unbuttoned her shirt, and he watched eagerly as she peeled it off, revealing her breasts.

"God," he said, reaching for them. He grasped them in his large hands, convulsively squeezing them.

"Easy!" she said as he mauled them, and then in a gentler tone she said, "Easy, Tom. You're very strong."

"I'm sorry."

He let her breasts just sit in his hands then and leaned over to mouth them, licking her nipples as she had his, and then sucking them gently.

"You can be a very gentle man when you want to be, can't you?"

"Do you like gentle men?"

"Sometimes," she said, closing her eyes as he continued to lick her breasts. She reached for his belt, undid it and pushed his pants so that they fell to the floor. He didn't have boots on and he kicked the pants away.

She got down on her knees, reached into his shorts and curled her fingers around his hugely erect organ.

"My God!" she said, only partially to please him. It was the most beautifully shaped penis she had ever seen, and nearly the largest. She put her lips over the head and began to wet it, licking and sucking it. She used the tip of her tongue to probe the slit of his penis, tasting his seminal fluid as it oozed slowly.

"Jesus, Liz," he said, and she opened her mouth wider and took as much of him inside as she could. She eased down his shorts and cupped his heavy balls in one hand while encircling the base of his penis with the other. Her head began to bob up and down, and his hips started to move, following her rhythm. As he neared orgasm she wanted to pull away so that she could take him in her pussy, but she found that she literally could not. It was as if her mouth had a mind of its own and wanted to suck his seed from him.

And then he came and filled her mouth in powerful spurts, moaning aloud as she continued to suck him, accommodating his entire emission. When she had swallowed the last of it she allowed him to slide from her mouth, still monstrously hard and erect.

"Where is your bed?" she asked breathlessly.

"This way," he replied in a voice as breathless as her own.

Joe Dunn waited in a doorway across the street, patiently smoking a cigarette.

Dunn knew who lived in the residential hotel over the way. He was familiar with most of the prominent people in San Francisco, who they were, where they lived, and what they did. He knew that Thomas Simonson — the nephew of Edward Simonson, one of *the* most prominent San Francisco citizens — lived in that hotel, and he assumed that this was whom Liz Archer had gone to see.

Tom Simonson was a big, good-looking young man who somehow managed to keep his name out of the papers. He didn't frequent casinos with women draped over his arm, or whorehouses, or Chinatown opium dens. He was the opposite of young Vincent Drake, which was probably why he was still alive and Drake was dead. Still, he *had* just been inside with Liz Archer for at least a half an hour, and what man could possibly resist a woman that beautiful?

Joe Dunn pondered a world that gave Simonson every advantage — a rich and powerful uncle, good looks, impending power — at such a young age, while he, Joe Dunn, honest lawman, was simply a policeman scrounging for whatever he could get. Shaking his head at the unfairness of it all, Joe stepped out of the doorway to stretch his legs and ease his muscles. As he did so, he presented his back to the man who had been moving up behind him. A perfect target for the wicked blade carried by a man named Hansen.

Simonson led Liz into the next room, walking ahead of her and affording her an admirable view of the play of muscles in his buttocks. In the bedroom they both stripped entirely and examined each other. A third party might have said that they made the perfect couple, because they were each the epitome of what the perfect man and woman should look like.

Tom was tall, broad-shouldered, slim-waisted, built like a Greek god. Even his organ was perfect. Liz was a golden goddess, with flawless breasts and hips, thighs and legs — what every woman wished she could look like.

They came together hotly, mouths avid, tongues seeking, finding, tasting each other. He was very different from Harry Lee, muscles bulging rather than taut. She ran her hands over his rock-like biceps, then slid them behind him so that she could cup his marble-like buttocks.

She found herself forgetting the original reason she had come here. Instead, she was fascinated by the perfection of his body. She fell to her knees and began to suckle him once again, licking his balls separately, and then quickly moving on to other parts of his body. She explored him with her mouth and hands, finally moving around behind him. She ran her tongue over his ass and probed between his buttocks as she reached in front of him and held his penis in both her hands.

Finally, as if he could take it no more, he came, spurting his seed out onto the floor while her tongue continued to poke at him. She used both hands to pump his penis, emptying it for the second time in minutes — and still it was hard!

"You're incredible," she said.

She'd had one man like Tom before — or rather the man had had her. That was Steve Madonna, in Diablo City, Texas. Madonna had been a pimp, though, breaking her in as his new whore. He had thoroughly fucked her and taught her everything she needed to know about pleasing a man, but *he* had controlled *her*, he had *taken* her. Now she was in the process of doing the same thing to young Tom Simonson.

Who seemed more than up to it.

"Up" was the word, for as she stood and moved around in front of him she could see that his penis was still incredibly erect. There was a pearl of semen on the tip, and she bent over to lick it off, then pushed him, trying to get him lying down. Instead, he lifted her easily in his arms and deposited her on the bed . . .

Hansen had been watching the policeman for a while, waiting for an opportunity to slip in behind him with his special blade. He had been waiting there for the woman and the lawman, and this was the first mistake the normally cautious Dunn had made.

A fatal one.

It was still fairly early in the day for city people, and the street was not busy. There was no one to see Hansen draw his blade, snake one arm around the lawman's neck from behind, pull his chin up and stretch his neck . . .

"Aren't you going to be late for work?"

"My uncle owns the place," Tom said. "Don't worry about that." His hands began to roam over her body, and he said in fascination, "You're so beautiful I can hardly believe it."

She ran both of her hands up his arms, squeezing his biceps and said, "I feel the same way about you. You're the perfect male, Tom."

"Liz," he said, leaning over to kiss her. His lips were gentle, his tongue insistent, pushing past her lips and teeth into her mouth. Fascinated by his penis she reached for it and gripped it with both hands.

"My turn," he said, disengaging her hands. She agreed, because even though it was his mouth that was now exploring her body, she felt that she was still in control.

The blood that soaked Hansen's sleeve didn't bother him. In fact, he enjoyed the sticky warmth. He kept his arm there even after he had felt the life go out of the lawman and used it to drag the man back into his doorway, where he released his hold and propped the man up against the door. The dead man looked just like someone answering a call of nature in a doorway.

Liz knew she wasn't in love with Tom Simonson, but he was so physically perfect that she lost track of everything else but the feel and taste of him.

As his tongue moved over her breasts, she rubbed her

palms over the muscles of his back. As he worked his way lower, kissing her belly, she wrapped her fingers in his thick hair. As his tongue reached her pubic patch and drove past it, entering her, she realized that he wasn't totally inexperienced. His tongue licked her vaginal lips, as he tasted her, then delved into her. She pressed her hips up against his mouth as his large, strong hands gripped her buttocks. When his tongue began to swirl around her clit she started to get dizzy and her stomach began to flutter. The orgasm rushed up on her and took hold of her so completely that she opened her mouth to cry out, but no sound came forth.

He was on top of her then, his huge organ inside of her, pounding in and then out as his breath rasped in her ear. He was heavy, but she didn't complain. She wrapped her arms and legs around his powerful body and held on while he continued to work his way to his own orgasm. For the first time she felt a vague disappointment as he came, filling her with his seed, because he was finished and out of her before she could achieve her second orgasm.

As he rolled off her, eyes closed and a dreamy smile on his face, he spoke one word that chilled her, bringing her back to reality.

Reverently he said, "Gabrielle."

CHAPTER TWENTY

"ALL RIGHT," Tom said, after they had rested for a few moments. "Ask your questions."

"I have to tell you the truth, Tom."

"What truth?"

"I don't work for the police," she said. "In fact, I don't even work with them."

"Who are you, then?"

"I'm being accused of having killed Vincent Drake, and I didn't do it. I'm trying to find out who did."

"Why didn't you say so in the first place?" he asked, turning onto his side so he could look at her. "I'll be happy to help you, Liz."

"Do you think that your uncle, or Gabrielle, could have killed him? Maybe to get back at him for something his father did? Or because he wouldn't marry Gabrielle?"

Tom thought for a moment and then said, "I think they're both capable of it, yes."

"But you don't know if they did it?"

"I don't know who did it, Liz," he said. "I do know one thing, though."

"What's that?"

"You didn't."

"How do you know that?"

"Because you just told me."

"No, I didn't," she said. "I said that I had to *prove* I wasn't guilty."

"That's good enough for me, Liz. I'll help you in any way I can."

"I appreciate that, Tom," Liz said gratefully. Then after a minute she asked, "Don't you have to get to work?"

"Yes, as a matter of fact, I do."

He rose and she watched as he dressed, the muscles of his finely sculptured body rippling as he moved. Much of her enjoyment in watching him was gone, however, because of the one word he had whispered after they'd made love.

Had Gabrielle Simonson been telling the truth, then? Had Tom Simonson learned what he knew about sex from his cousin?

"Just pull the door closed when you leave, Liz," Tom said, leaning over to kiss her. She smiled and offered her mouth.

"I will."

"Or stay until I come back," he added, straightening up.

"I can't," she said. "I have to go and see Vincent Drake's brother and sister."

He made a face and said, "That'll be unpleasant."

"Maybe, but they're probably the only ones I haven't spoken to yet."

"I hope it helps," he said. "The faster we clear you,

the faster we can get on with our lives.''

''Tom — ''

''I have to hurry, honey,'' he said, moving toward the door. ''I'll see you later.''

''All right, Tom.''

He was out of the room and then out of the place completely before she could call him back. ''Get on with our lives,'' he'd said. Was he still young and naive enough to think that sex with a woman other than his cousin meant love?

And what would Gabrielle Simonson do once she heard about this from him?

As Simonson reached the lobby, the clerk called out to him.

''Mr. Simonson!''

''Yeah, Seth?''

''Was it all right?'' the clerk asked nervously.

''Was what all right, Seth?''

''To let the young lady go on up.''

''Sure, Seth,'' Simonson said, patting the clerk on the shoulder. ''It was real fine.''

Liz rested for a few more minutes, then rose and got dressed slowly. Fully dressed, she then searched both rooms, being careful not to leave them looking as if they had been searched.

She found nothing, but then she didn't know what she was looking for. Maybe something that would tell her if Tom had had anything to do with Vincent Drake's murder. There was nothing of that sort to be found, however, and she gave up.

She walked to the window in the sitting room, but it

overlooked an alley and not the main street. From there she couldn't tell if Joe Dunn was outside, although she was pretty sure he was.

She wondered what he thought she had been doing for the past hour. Or if he cared.

She found a basin of water and, dampening a towel, cleaned the floor where Tom had spilled his seed. As she prepared to leave she found herself hoping that she would be able to convince Tom that their involvement was purely physical, because she very much wanted to get physical with Tom Simonson again — more than once, if possible — before leaving San Francisco. Next time she'd have to slow him down so that they could both experience the satisfaction they deserved.

Hansen was standing in the doorway with the dead man when Tom Simonson stepped out of the hotel, paused a moment to look around and then started off down the street.

Hansen backed out of the doorway, made sure that the dead man still looked as if he were taking a leak against the door, and then started across the street to the hotel to take care of the rest of the business that Wilkes had sent him there for.

CHAPTER TWENTY-ONE

As LIZ LEFT Simonson's suite she felt a chill, as if it had suddenly become colder. Tate Gilmore had often told her that "feelings" saved more lives than anything else.

Unless it was caution.

She might not have chosen to go out the back door if she hadn't thought about Gilmore, but *not* thinking about Tate Gilmore was almost unheard of.

Instead of heading for the steps to the lobby, she turned left and walked toward the other end of the hall. Sure enough, there was a back stairway, and she took it down to the rear door and out into the alley that ran alongside the hotel.

Hansen knew exactly where he was going. He marched through the lobby, and the clerk didn't have the courage to question him. He went up to the second-floor hall and walked directly to number sixteen. He let himself in and, when he found the rooms empty, cursed and hurried back out.

Liz reached the front of the hotel and looked across the street, checking doorways. She was looking for Joe Dunn. When she finally spotted him, she hurried across, hoping that he would finish what he was doing before she reached him, to avoid embarrassment for both of them. Unfortunately, he still had his back turned as she reached the doorway. She could have waited, but that chill still pervaded the air around her, and she wanted to let Dunn know.

"Mr. Dunn," she said, touching his shoulder. When he didn't answer or turn around she grasped his shoulder harder, ready to call his name again. He started to fall back toward her, and she instinctively jumped away, causing him to fall at her feet. She saw the gaping wound in his throat, and her breath caught in her own.

She turned, her first thought to go back into the hotel. That was where she'd find Joe Dunn's killer, she figured. But Tate Gilmore's advice sprang to mind again. She wasn't on her own ground, and the killer probably was. Caution dictated that she move on. She would find a policeman and report Dunn's death. Eventually, that would bring Inspector Granger running. She needed to talk to him again, anyway.

Hansen came rushing out the front door hoping to catch sight of the blonde woman, but all he saw was the dead man lying half in and half out of the doorway. Before long somebody would see him and start raising hell. He decided to report back to Wilkes that things had not gone exactly as planned—but then when did they ever? At least the lawman was out of the way. The girl would be next.

CHAPTER TWENTY-TWO

"TELL IT TO ME AGAIN."

"Don't be mad at me, Granger," Liz said. "You're the one who sent him to keep an eye on me . . . alone. If he'd watched me as well as he watched himself I'd be dead, too."

If it hadn't been for the chill she'd felt that had sent her out the back door, maybe she would have been dead — or maybe she would have seen who killed poor Joe Dunn.

"All right," Granger said wearily. "Would you tell it to me again . . . please?"

She told it to him again. She had come to see Thomas Simonson, she *had* seen him —

"And he left you in his suite, alone," Granger interrupted.

"Yes."

"Why?"

She smiled and said, "He had to go to work."

"And you had to get dressed?"

She didn't answer.

He shrugged and said, "All right, go on."

She told him that when she left Simonson's rooms she decided to use the back door.

"Why?"

"Just a feeling I had."

"About what?"

She shrugged.

"I just didn't feel like going out the front door."

"Is that some kind of instinct for danger you gun people have?"

"Gun people?"

"You know, like the dime novels say? Gunfighters have an instinct for danger — "

"Don't tell me you believe that. That's just in the dime novels, isn't it, Inspector?"

They were in Granger's office at headquarters, and he stood up from behind his desk now.

"Well, something kept you from walking into the arms of a killer, Miss Archer. I'd be very interested to know what it was."

"So would I."

Granger stared at her in silence for a few moments, then slammed his open palm against his desk with a resounding bang that must have hurt.

"Joe Dunn was my friend," he said, rubbing his hand. "He was a good lawman. I want the person who killed him, Miss Archer."

"I don't blame you, Inspector," she said, sympathetically. "I want him, too, because *he's* probably the one who killed Vincent Drake."

"Do you have any proof of that?"

"No, but do you really need any? You know I didn't kill either of them, don't you?"

"My chief needs proof, Miss Archer," he said, and she was afraid she knew what that meant.

"And that's what I want to get him."

"By stumbling around in a city that you're unfamiliar with?"

"Well, I'm not going to find out by sitting in one of your cells, am I?"

"There would be a lot less pressure on me if that's where you were."

She knew she had to do some fast talking to stay out of jail.

"If you put me in a cell they won't be able to try to kill me again."

"Is that what you want to be?" he asked. "A piece of bait?"

"Let's stop kidding around, Inspector," Liz said dryly. "Isn't that why you let me escape in the first place?"

"*Let* you escape?" he asked, trying to look outraged. "Who told you that?"

"Give me credit for *some* brains, Inspector. Nobody had to tell me."

He glared at her for a few seconds and then said, "I'm going to need an alibi for you if I'm going to let you go. I've got to justify it."

"Can't you just let me escape again?"

"I thought you wanted me to give you some credit for brains?"

"That wouldn't look good, huh?"

"I'd be out of the force in no time," he said, shaking his head. "And believe me that's the last thing I want."

"Thomas Simonson," she said after a few moments. "He'll give me an alibi."

"Are you sure?"

"Why?"

"What if he's the one who set you up for this?"

"For what?"

"To be killed. Or to be blamed for Joe Dunn's murder."

"How could he have set me up? He didn't know I was coming to see him this morning."

"He could have guessed," Granger said. "For instance, when I let you out of here I'm willing to bet that you'll go straight to see Vincent Drake's brother and sister."

She started to reply, then stopped herself. He was right, and there was no point in denying it.

"We're back to square one," he said. "You need an alibi."

"Find Simonson," she said. "If he is the one who set me up, then he'd want me out to try again, wouldn't he?"

"You'll still have to wait in a cell."

She was trying to think of an alternative when there was a knock on his door. A uniformed policeman entered, spoke briefly to Granger in low tones, went out again and returned several moments later with someone in tow.

Harry Lee.

"Harry," Granger said.

Harry nodded, then looked at Liz. "Are you all right?"

"I'm fine, Harry," she said. "I'm just in need of a good alibi."

Harry looked at Granger. "How good an alibi am I?"

"You weren't even there, Harry," Granger said wearily.

Harry shrugged. "Who knows that except you, me and Liz? I'll swear she was with me all morning. What more do you need from a witness?"

Granger sat down in his chair and rubbed his hands over his face.

"All right, get out of here, both of you."

"Are you going to put another man on her?"

"I had my best man on her," Granger said. "And *he* got careless."

"Who's the best man you've got now?" Harry Lee asked.

Granger looked at him. "I am."

"Well," Harry said, "I'll stay with her until you can break away from here, Inspector."

"What makes you think — ?"

They were heading for the door, and Harry said, "Steelman will go along with anything you want to do, Dan. You know that."

"I wish I was as sure as you are," Granger said to the closing door. "I wish I was as sure."

CHAPTER TWENTY-THREE

"How did you know I was in there?"

"I was outside when they brought you in."

Liz stared at Harry and said, "You waited a long time before coming in."

"I wanted to see if you could get yourself out, first," he told her. "It's not an easy thing for me to walk into that place, you know."

"Do you know where Pacific Avenue is?"

"Of course."

"That's where Vincent Drake's brother and sister are staying."

"No wonder their father won't have anything to do with them."

"Why?"

"That's a bad area, Liz."

"Take me there, will you?"

"Sure," he said. "We can walk."

On the way, Liz said curiously, "You called the inspector 'Dan,' Harry. I didn't know you were on a first-name basis with him."

"Mostly I'm not."

"Why at all?"

"We grew up down here together," Harry said. "Oh, he's a few years older than I am, and he left after a while to work for the Pinks, but he came back first chance he got."

"You're not friends?"

"We're a little too far apart in our beliefs for that," Harry said. "I guess we're somewhere in the middle ground between friends and adversaries."

"Terrible place to be."

"Where?" he asked, frowning.

"In the middle."

"A what?"

"A leave of absence," Granger said.

"What for?"

"I need a rest."

"You're full of shit, Dan!" Steelman said.

"Maybe."

"You're running a game on me, Dan," Steelman said. "That's what got you fired by Allan Pinkerton."

"I didn't get fired — "

"I know," Steelman said. "You and Allan mutually agreed that you should leave."

"Can I have my leave?"

"You know what I think?"

"Yes," Granger said. "Can I have my leave?"

"Get out of here," Steelman said. "When can I expect you back?"

"A week. Maybe two," Granger said. "Or whenever my leave is finished. Whichever comes first."

"Thanks for giving me something I can count on."

"This is it," Harry Lee said, gazing up at a four-story building that looked as though a good stiff wind would knock it clean over.

"What is it?" Liz asked.

"A hotel. Kind of."

"Kind of?"

"You going in?"

"Yes."

"You'll see."

"You're not going in?"

"No, I'll wait out here, keep an eye out."

"For what?"

"For whatever."

She nodded and went inside.

"What room are the Drakes in?"

"Could be in his," the wizened old clerk said unconcernedly. "Or could be in hers."

"Well then, could you give me their room numbers?"

"What I look like, some kind of information service?"

"You look like an old man who's going to be eating what he's got left of his teeth if he doesn't answer my question."

He narrowed his eyes at her and said, "Think you're tough, do you?"

"I'm tougher than you," Liz said curtly. "That's all you need to know right now."

He thought about it for a few moments, then said, "You

might try room five. If they ain't in there you might try
room seven.''

"Thank you."

As she turned to walk to the stairs the front door opened
and a woman walked in with a man, a sailor from all appearances. Her hand was down the front of his pants, and
he was grinning stupidly. Liz let them go up the stairs ahead
of her, and then followed.

Kind of a hotel.

She found the door to room five ajar. She knocked and
entered, but the room was empty. The bed was unmade
and there were whiskey bottles on the floor next to it. There
was an odor in the air that she could not identify, never
having smelled opium before. She was about to leave and
try room seven when she saw that a door in the far wall
was also ajar. She approached it and was about to knock
when she heard sounds from the other side. Moaning and
sighing sounds that were all too familiar to her.

It seemed there was a connecting door between rooms
five and seven. Liz pushed it open a few more inches, so
she could peer in.

A naked man was standing with his right side to her. On
the floor in front of him was a woman on her knees, licking the length of his long, thin penis. As Liz watched, the
woman squeezed the man's balls and took the bulbous
head of his cock into her mouth. The man moaned appreciatively. He appeared to be in his late twenties and in fair
shape, though somewhat pale. The woman, who seemed
younger, was full-bodied to the point of voluptuousness.
Her buttocks and breasts were full and firm. She would
have looked right in a frame hanging over a bar in some

saloon for men to ogle. A woman built for ogling . . . and for bedding.

Liz pulled the door closed and backed away, leaving the room. In the hall she walked to the door of room seven and knocked loudly. From inside there came a long, shuddering moan and she knew it would be a few moments before her knock was answered.

When the door opened, the man and woman were standing side by side. He was wearing his pants and the woman was wearing a robe and holding onto his left arm. They both looked flushed and somewhat dazed.

"Yes?"

"I'm looking for either David Drake or Vivien Drake."

The man smiled and said, "I'm David Drake." Then, indicating the woman who had been sucking his cock only moments before, he said, "And this is my sister, Vivien. How can we help you?"

CHAPTER TWENTY-FOUR

FIGHTING OFF her shock, Liz said, "I'd like to talk to you about your brother, Vincent."

"Ah, our dear, departed brother," David Drake said. "Were you one of his, ah, playmates?"

"No," Liz said. "I'm working with the police on his killing. May I come in?"

"Certainly," David said, backing away, and moving Vivien along with him. "We can take it if you can."

Liz wasn't sure what he meant, but she entered the room and closed the door behind them. The door connecting the two rooms was still ajar.

Brother and sister retreated to the bed. Vivien sat down on it, and David stood near it.

"I gather you weren't very close to your brother?" Liz asked.

"Our brother, our father," David said. "We're not very close to anyone."

"Except each other," Vivien said, speaking for the first time. Liz saw that her face was a bit chubby, but she had beautiful, long chestnut hair and her voice was deep and sexy. Her hand was on her brother's thigh.

"Of course," he agreed.

"Do you have any idea who might have wanted to kill Vincent?"

"Lots of people," David said.

"Father, for one," Vivien said.

"What about you?"

David laughed and Vivien smiled.

"We had little use for Vincent, although he did understand us better than our father does. Not that he approved, of course. Anyway, we had no reason to kill Vincent. He went his way and we went ours."

"And none of you went your father's way?"

"Our father likes to live on Nob Hill and flaunt his money and power," David said. "We have some money of our own, but we prefer living here. It's closer to the way we feel about life."

"And Vincent?"

"Vincent felt more the way we do than the way our father does," David said. "That was why he got his enjoyment from whorehouses in Chinatown. We don't need that sort of satisfaction."

"I see."

"Do you?" David asked, eyeing her appreciatively.

"The door to room five was left open," she told him. He looked at the connecting door, and then seemed to understand. He didn't look at all embarrassed. Vivien didn't appear even to know what they were talking about. From the sleepy look in her eyes Liz figured she was either drunk or drugged. She kept running her hand up and down the back of her brother's thigh.

"Do we shock you?" David asked Liz.

"Yes," she answered honestly. She didn't add that they disgusted her, as well, and made her think of Gabrielle and Thomas Simonson, who were only cousins.

"We know what we are, Miss . . . ?"

"Archer."

"We know what we are," David said, again. "We are sensualists, and we've known since we were children that only we can satisfy each other's wants and needs. We're honest about it, which is more than some people are about their . . . needs."

"I suppose you have a point," Liz said. "Is there nothing you can tell me that might help us figure out who killed your brother?"

"Only that we are rich," David said. "That is, the Drakes — our father, Vincent when he was alive, and ourselves. We have money, and some people don't like that."

"Are you saying that someone might have killed your brother simply out of envy?"

"It's possible, isn't it?"

"It might be," Liz said, not meaning it. Considering what had happened to Joe Dunn and a Chinese whore Liz had never met, she doubted it.

"And now if you would excuse us," David said, unbuckling his pants, "my sister and I have some unfinished business."

Liz didn't think the man would do it, but he dropped his pants right in front of her, revealing his long, rigid organ. His sister, her eyes glistening, wet her lips and reached for his cock to fondle it lovingly.

David looked at Liz with frankness and said, "You're very beautiful. Would you care to join us?"

"I — no," Liz stammered.

David shrugged. He looked at his sister, undid her robe so that her big breasts dangled free and then leaned over to capture one cherry nipple in his mouth while her fist began to stroke him up and down. They began to moan and sigh, almost in unison.

Liz, realizing that the scene held a sort of perverse fascination for her, turned and groped blindly for the door. She couldn't see or breathe. She knew she had to get out of the room before she passed out.

Outside the hotel she found Harry Lee still waiting for her.

"What happened?" he asked, seeing the look on her face and the pasty white color of her skin.

She opened her mouth to answer and suddenly she couldn't. She found herself gagging, and staggered off the boardwalk to an alley, as bile spewed forth from her mouth uncontrollably. She coughed and choked as the bile burned her nose and throat. When she was finished, she spat one final time and wiped her mouth on her sleeve.

"Liz?"

"Take me someplace where we can get some coffee," she said in a raspy voice.

"Want to wash away the taste of bile?" he asked, solicitously.

"That's not all!"

CHAPTER TWENTY-FIVE

OVER COFFEE Liz told him what she had seen. Harry Lee showed no shock or surprise.

"Incest is a rich man's pleasure," he said, as if that explained it away. "You won't find that among the poor wretches of Chinatown, only on Nob Hill. We have more respect for family than to bed our own sisters."

Liz decided not to tell him that it looked as though the sister was as eager as the brother. Instead, she shook her head, unable to understand it.

"What are you going to do next?" Harry asked. "There's no policeman on our tail, you know. I think Granger has put you out to dry."

"I'll just have to wait for them to make a try at me," she said.

"And if they don't kill you, then what?"

"I'll have to take somebody alive, so I can prove I'm innocent."

"I don't know if you're going to take the man with the blade alive," Harry Lee said doubtfully. "He gets in close to do his work. The only way you're going to get away from him is to kill him."

"Unless he decides to do it with a bullet."

"Which could come from a rooftop. You'd never even see it."

"That's a possibility," she admitted, pouring herself another cup of coffee.

They were silent for a few moments, and then Harry spoke.

"I have an idea."

"What?"

"You've talked to everyone you can possibly talk to. Now you've just got to wait." He leaned forward, putting his elbows on the table. "Why wait for them out in the open?" he asked.

"What do you mean?"

"I mean I know a place where you can wait — "

"I don't want to be inaccessible," she said, interrupting him. "I don't want to make it too hard."

"Or too easy," he added. "Don't worry. The place I have in mind you won't be too inaccessible, at all."

First they went to find Carla, then to pick up something special for Liz, and then Carla and Harry took Liz to Madam Chou's on Ross Alley. As soon as they entered, Liz knew what he meant by not being inaccessible.

He looked at her and shrugged.

"Well, while you're here you will have to act the part," he said.

"Will I?" she asked. "Well, it wouldn't exactly be the first time."

"Let's talk to Madam Chou."

As it turned out, it was Carla, who knew Madam Chou, who explained that they wanted to hide Liz there for a while.

"Why is he here?" Madam Chou asked, looking at Harry Lee. "Is she his woman?"

"No," Carla said. "My brother is here as a favor to me, Madam Chou, not for the tong."

The older woman eyed Harry dubiously, then looked Liz up and down.

"The other girls will be jealous of her if she doesn't work," she said.

Carla looked at Liz, who nodded without hesitation.

"She will work," Carla said.

"She'll add some class to the place," Harry added, and that drew him a look of scorn from the madam. She thought all of her girls were classy.

"She will need some clothes."

"I brought some," Carla said, putting down the leather valise she had been carrying. She looked at Liz, eyes glittering mischievously and said, "I had to guess at your size, but I had a pretty good idea."

"This was not an idea that just occurred to you this morning," Liz said, looking at Harry Lee.

"Carla and I discussed it last night."

"How," Liz began and then, looking at Madam Chou, phrased the remainder of her question carefully, "will they know where I am?"

"I'll make sure it's an open secret."

Liz frowned. She wanted to ask Harry Lee if he thought he knew who the killer was, but she didn't want to do it in front of Madam Chou.

Madam Chou looked at Carla and said, "And you,

Carla? Are you ready to come back to work for me?''

"No, Madam Chou," Carla answered without hesitation.

Madam Chou looked at Liz and said, "I will have someone show you your room. You will have to work," she said again, "or my other girls won't like it."

"I'll work, Madam Chou," Liz assured her. "For the short time I'll be here."

"And I might even know who your first customer will be," Harry Lee said, smiling.

"Are you gonna tell your boss?" Hansen asked Wilkes.

"No," Wilkes said. "And he's your boss, too."

"I'm taking his money," Hansen admitted. "But he ain't *my* boss."

"Sure."

"Are you afraid of him?" Hansen asked.

"No," Wilkes said, looking annoyed. "I'm just afraid to have to do without his money."

That Hansen could understand.

"No, we're not gonna tell him anything until that girl is dead."

"Which will be soon," Hansen said, confidently.

"Sure, if she hasn't gone underground," Wilkes said. "Now she knows somebody's after her — "

Hansen was shaking his head, and Wilkes stopped.

"What's the matter with you?"

"She's trying to clear her name, right?"

"So?"

"So the three of us are the only ones who *know* that she didn't kill the Drake kid. You think she hasn't known all along that we'd make a try for her?"

Wilkes stared at Hansen with something like awe. The

killer never talked very much, so Wilkes was surprised to hear him reason something out that way.

"So?" he asked again, looking at the big man with interest. He had heard much about the man called Swede Hansen along the Barbary Coast, but he had never heard that the man had brains.

"So even if she has gone underground, she'll find a way to let us know where she is."

Wilkes thought it over and said, "That makes sense."

"And when we find out where she is," Hansen said, taking out his blade and running his thumb along the edge —drawing blood in the process— "we'll go and get her."

That made sense, too.

When Carla returned to her room there was a man there waiting for her. As he turned the lamp up she started and caught her breath.

"Wha — ?"

"It's only me."

She peered through the dim light and said, "I didn't recognize you."

"I don't wonder," he replied. "Did you get Liz safely stashed away?"

"How did you know?"

"I know your brother, Carla," the man said. "Are you going to tell me where she is?"

"Well," Carla said, moving across the room toward him. "Of course."

CHAPTER TWENTY-SIX

A WHORE named Willi — the only black girl in Madam Chou's stable — showed Liz to her room so she could change. As Liz entered, Willi walked in behind her and shut the door.

"Hope you don't mind if I watch," Willi said, sitting on the bed. "Just sizing up the competition."

"I don't mind," Liz said, starting to undress. She was no longer self-conscious about undressing around another woman. Carla had helped her with that.

Willi was tall and lean, with small breasts that were nevertheless pushed up to accent their roundness. What Liz noticed most about the girl, though, was her behind. It was big and round and firm, and when she walked she stuck it out and moved it around.

"Wow, you've got nice ones," Willi said, examining and admiring Liz's naked breasts with clinical interest.

"If I had a pair like that I wouldn't have to work my ass so much."

"Work your ass?"

"Sure," the girl said. "You know. A man sees a girl with big breasts and he wants to play with them, stick his meat between them, you know. Me, all they want me to do is get down on all fours so they can play with my ass."

Liz pulled her dress on and found it cut daringly low. Carla had bought her something that would really show her off to her best advantage — and possibly cause her to catch cold, too.

"Golly, you're beautiful," the girl said.

"Thanks," Liz said. "Tell me, do all the girls here see each other as competition?"

"I can see you ain't put in much time in a whorehouse," Willi said.

"Not that much," Liz admitted.

"Well, the more you get picked the more money you make," Willi pointed out. "I mean, the harder you work, too; but you've got to work hard if you want to make money."

"Makes sense."

"So we all dress up to show off what we got. Me, my ass; Rachel, her huge breasts; you — well, honey, you got everything, which ain't gonna make you real popular with a lot of the other girls."

"I'm not looking to step on anyone's toes, Willi."

"You can't help but do that, honey," Willi said, standing up.

"What about you?" Liz asked. "Why are you so friendly?"

"Hell, I'm just a friendly gal, Liz."

"Tell me something, Willi?"

"Sure. What?"

"I heard Madam Chou ask Carla Lee if she was ready to come back to work for her."

"That was before my time," Willi said. "But I've heard some of the other girls talk about Carla Lee. She's supposed to have been Madam Chou's best girl ever."

"I see."

"Come on," Willi said, starting for the door. "I'll introduce you around to the other girls. You might as well know who your enemies are."

"I'll be along in a minute, okay?"

"Sure. See you downstairs."

Liz had reluctantly left her gun with Harry Lee rather than wear it into the whorehouse, because who would believe a gun-toting whore? Instead, they had stopped off to pick up a two-shot derringer which, now that Willi was gone, Liz took out of Carla's valise and tucked into the top of her stocking.

Before she left the room she picked up one more item: the orange bandana given to her by Tate Gilmore. It was her good-luck charm, even more so than the little metal ace of spades that Chance Taker had given her. That she left in the room; but the bandana she'd worn during every gun battle she'd been in was tucked carefully down the bodice of her dress, between her breasts.

Now she was ready to go down and meet the girls.

CHAPTER TWENTY-SEVEN

WHEN WILKES walked into the Barbary Coast saloon he and Hansen had agreed to meet at, he spotted his temporary partner lingering over a beer. He stopped at the bar for a beer of his own, then carried it to the table and sat down opposite Hansen.

"Nothing," he said morosely. "If we don't find her soon — " he started. Then he noticed the look on Hansen's face and stopped.

"Something?" he asked.

"Something," Hansen said, smiling. "I found her."

The girls were named Mimi and Candy and Delores, and Li, Tan and Ana, and Willi and Liz, but Liz Archer forgot their names moments after she was introduced. She ignored the daggers that were coming from their eyes because they all knew she was the loveliest woman there. After three days the only thing Liz did remember was meeting Rachel of the huge breasts, which she showed off in a filmy, clingy, low-cut nightie. In five years, Liz recalled thinking, they would be down to her *knees*.

She took her place on one of the overstuffed sofas and watched as the regular customers came and went, picking their usual girls. She really had no intention of "working," only of appearing willing to work. The few times strangers considered picking her, she was able to dissuade them with a well-chosen word or two. She told one man that she hoped he wouldn't mind if she wasn't exactly *well*, but that she would try her best.

"Boy, I'm surprised," Willi said halfway through the night, seating herself next to Liz.

"About what?"

"About you," the black girl said.

"What do you mean?"

"I thought you'd have been up and down those stairs so many times by now you'd have musclebound legs."

Liz shrugged and said, "Guess I haven't struck anybody's fancy."

"Bull!"

"What?"

"You been shooin' them away, girl. I been watchin' you. Oh, don't worry, I ain't gonna tell Madam Chou."

"Tell her what?"

"That you ain't a real whore."

"I haven't brought in any money in three days," Liz said, "so I guess she knows that already."

"Not yet. She gives her girls some time to get comfortable. A couple more days, though, and you might be out of a job."

"A couple more days," Liz said, "is all it will take, I hope."

"All what will take?"

Liz looked at Willi and said, "For me to get comfortable."

"Oh, you're waitin' for more than that, girl."

"Willi —"

"Don't worry, Liz," the other girl said, holding up her hands. "I'm not gonna get nosy. Curious, yes, but not nosy."

At that point a man who had been coming for the past three nights entered, and Willi saw him.

"There's my new customer," she said, hastily getting to her feet. "He's a live one. I won't be seeing you for the rest of the night, Liz."

"Have fun."

Willie took a step and then stopped and turned to face Liz again.

"You know, eventually you're gonna get one that you can't scare off. What will you do then?"

Liz shrugged and said, "Go to work, I guess."

Willi hurried over to her man and, for the fourth time in four nights, Liz couldn't help feeling that there was something familiar about him, although it certainly wasn't his oversized nose. Maybe it was the way he moved, she thought, as they went up the stairs arm in arm to Willi's room.

She forgot about them, however, when Harry Lee entered. He spotted her and walked over to her.

"Are you free?"

"Nothing," she said, standing up and giving him a saucy look, "is free, mister — least of all in here."

Wilkes and Hansen entered Ross Alley after midnight.

"We go in together?" Hansen asked.

"No," Wilkes said. "I'll go in first. You wait fifteen minutes and then come in and pick her out. I'll be upstairs when you get there with her."

"All right," Hansen said. "Am I gonna get to . . . enjoy her?"

"Just kill her, don't play any games."

"I wasn't talking about before I killed her," Hansen said, grinning. "I meant after."

"You're the strangest man," Willi told her customer after they had closed the door behind them in her room. "All you want to do is sit in here and wait, every night for the past four nights. What are you waiting for?"

He looked at her and said, "Trouble."

"Well, you sure don't do a lot for a girl's ego."

The first night he had come she had stripped naked for him, preening in front of him, pinching her dark, chocolate-brown nipples and presenting her best asset — her ass — to him, but he had showed very little interest beyond an obvious bulge in his pants.

"At least I know you ain't queer," she said, " 'cause every time I undress for you your meat stands up straight and tall."

She removed her dress and stood before him, lean and naked, small breasts cupped in her hands. He stared at her and the bulge appeared in his pants, right on schedule.

"It's got nothing to do with you, Willi," he said. "Believe me, I'd like nothing better than to get in bed with you . . ."

"But?"

"I can't, not right now."

"Well, we wouldn't really have to get into bed, you know," she said, approaching the chair he was seated in.

She came right up against him so that he could feel the heat radiating from her body. "In fact, you wouldn't even have to get undressed. I'm really very good, and I'm just dying to show you." She leaned over him from behind, full lips against his ear and said, "What do you say?"

"Word has gotten out, so I can't stay long," Harry Lee said.

"Harry, when we first came here it occurred to me that you might know who the killer is." When he didn't reply, Liz asked, "Do you?"

Harry hesitated, then said, "I might."

"How?"

"The weapon he used."

"A knife?"

"Not just any knife," Harry said. "The way Drake and Dunn and . . . and the Chinese whore were skewered, it's more than just a knife. It's a special kind of knife."

"Then you do know who it is," Liz said excitedly. Something dawned on her then, and she said, "But if you know who he is from the weapon he used, then so must Granger — if he's a good lawman."

"Oh, he's a good lawman, all right."

"Then you both know."

"We both think we know," Harry said. "But what you want is the man behind him."

"What I want is the killer, because that would prove that I'm not."

"All right. You want the killer. Granger wants the man behind him."

"What do you want, Harry?"

A funny look came over his face and he said, "I want . . I want to help you, Liz."

She didn't belive that, but she didn't press him, either. Whatever his reason the fact remained that he *was* helping her, and she was prepared to accept that.

"You're going to have to work tonight," he said then.

"Why?"

"Because if he shows up tonight he's going to pick you. Don't try to put him off."

"If he's the killer," she said, "I won't be able to put him off, no matter what I say."

"Do you have your gun?"

"No," she said. "I don't have *my* gun. You have that. All I have is this little peashooter."

"Well," he said, producing her gun from inside his coat, "now you have yours. Hide it up here where you can get at it."

"Oh, it'll be right where I can get at it," she said, taking it and placing it under her pillow, "while I'm working."

CHAPTER TWENTY-EIGHT

HARRY LEE LEFT Liz's room and went back downstairs. Instead of leaving, however, he went to Madam Chou's office and walked in without knocking.

"Can I help you?" the woman asked from behind her desk.

"I am going to be around for a while tonight, Madam Chou," he said. "I just wanted to let you know."

"I have made my monthly payment to the tong—" she began, but he waved her off.

"I am not here for the tong," he said. "I am here for myself."

"Why?"

"You'll find out soon enough," he said. "You have a peephole in here, I believe."

Madam Chou frowned and said, "Who told you —?"

"No one had to tell me. Where is it?"

She pointed to a cabinet set against the wall. He walked

to it, opened the door and found the hole. Through it he could see her sitting room. As he watched, Liz Archer came back downstairs and made herself comfortable on one of the oversized sofas.

"This will be fine," Harry Lee said. "Just go on about your business, Madam Chou. Don't mind me."

"See?" Willi said to her customer. "You don't even have to get undressed."

She had opened his pants, reached in, and worked his huge tool out. It was a lovely thing, so lovely that she wondered why he didn't want to get undressed. Could it be that he had some kind of scar on his body that he was ashamed of?

"You just relax, baby," she said, flicking her tongue out to lick the crown of his cock. "Let me do all the work."

As she opened her mouth and swooped down on his rigid organ, taking it between her talented lips, she knew that the last thing her customer would be able to do was relax.

Not with little Willi working her magic on his meat.

Liz kept her eyes on the door for the remainder of the night, watching all of the men who entered. They all seemed to be regulars, going upstairs with their regular girls, and the one man who seemed to be a stranger took the first girl he saw, which was Rachel. He must have been in a hurry.

True to her word, Liz had not seen Willi since she had gone upstairs with her customer, the man who was somehow familiar to her. Allowed to think about it a little longer, she might have realized who he was, but suddenly a man entered the place, looked around and stopped when his eyes fell on Liz. He crossed the room to her, and her heart began to pound.

This could be it!

Harry saw the man walk up to Liz, and drew his breath in.

His guess had been right, but he found no great pleasure in the fact. They were dealing with a man who had no scruples, who killed without a second thought.

The man he knew only as Hansen was possibly the most dangerous man on the Barbary Coast, and he had to allow Liz to go upstairs with him.

Alone.

Willi felt the man's cock expand and his balls swell just before he began to shoot into her mouth. She moaned appreciatively and swallowed all of his seed. She loved sucking men, if only because it gave her a chance to rest her ass, which, on a normal night, became pretty sore.

The man groaned aloud, and his legs shot straight out as he emptied himself into her mouth. She placed her hands on his thighs and squeezed him tightly, sucking him dry, and then released him with a smile.

"See?" she said. "I knew you liked me."

"Willi — "

"There are a lot of things we can do without undressing you," she told him, sliding into his lap. She pressed her chocolate nipples to his mouth, eliciting a tentative tongue, and then prodded his ear with her tongue and wiggled her ass in his lap. She was surprised and delighted to find him responding. She could feel his cock swelling beneath her ass cheeks.

"Tell me, " she said, whispering into his ear, "have you ever eaten a black girl?"

"N-never."

"Would you like to?"

"Willi — "

In an even hoarser whisper she said, full lips right up against his ear, "You don't even have to get undressed."

She felt him waver and slid off his lap quickly, before he could change his mind.

She grabbed his hand, pulling him from the chair to the bed and saying, "Come on, baby. Willi needs a little attention."

"Are you busy?" the man asked her.

She stood up to face him and said, "Not for you."

He looked her over, and she found herself looking into a pair of the coldest eyes she'd ever seen.

"All right, then," he said, "let's go upstairs."

He was a big man, broad-shouldered, blunt-featured . . . and cold. She had no doubt that he was the killer. A man like this would only know one thing to do with a woman — kill her.

"Come with me," she said. She reached for his hand, but he pulled it away, as if he wanted to keep his hands free.

Yes, this is him, she thought, leading him to the stairs.

The gun under her pillow seemed very far away.

Willi had the man lying on his back in bed, and she was straddling his head, bringing her juicy pussy closer and closer to his face. The fragrance was too much for him to resist, and he reached out with his tongue to lick the length of her slick lips, up and down and up again, each lick more avid than the one before.

"Well," she said, her eyes closed as she rejoiced in the

feel of his tongue, moving her hips in the opposite direction to his licking motion. "It looks like Willi finally got you interested!"

Harry watched carefully through the peephole as Liz led Hansen up the steps. Then he hurried from the room to follow them up.

Madam Chou stared after him. She did not know what was going to happen, but she knew that trouble was brewing, and she just knew it had to have something to do with the death of the young master, Drake, and of her girl, Ling.

She had been wondering how long it would take for her involvement in that to come back and haunt her.

CHAPTER TWENTY-NINE

LIZ LED THE BIG MAN to her room and opened the door, thinking only of the gun under her pillow. The two-shot derringer on her thigh would be no use against a man his size, unless she could hit him just right.

As she entered the room she suddenly felt his big hand against her back. Then he propelled her forward so hard that her head jerked back from the force of the push. She tripped over the edge of the bed and went sprawling on the floor.

He advanced on her before she had a chance to get to her feet and reached down. Her dress had hiked up around her hips and he plucked the derringer from her thigh.

"What were you planning to do with this, little lady?" he asked. The gun looked like a toy in his big hand.

"Just self-defense," she said. "Some customers get kind of rough, you know?"

"Sure, I know," he said, straightening up so that he

looked over her. She chanced a glance at the bed, where her gun was hidden beneath the pillow. She'd have to get past him to get at it.

He tossed the derringer aside and drew a wickedly long blade from a leather sheath he'd had hidden in his pants. It wasn't quite a saber, but it was bigger and deadlier-looking than a bowie knife.

She had seen what that knife had done to two men, and her stomach knotted.

As Wilkes entered the room with Rachel, she turned and dropped her nightie to give him a good look at her huge breasts. She wiggled her shoulders, set her breasts rippling and said, "Like 'em?"

Most men jumped her at that point, desperately trying to get as much of her as they could into their mouths. She tensed for the attack, but got more than she bargained for.

"You look like a damned cow," Wilkes said, and back-handed her across the mouth. Her head shot back and her eyes went blank as she fell backwards on to the floor.

Wilkes liked his women lean and slim.

He moved to the door, opened it a crack and waited. After about ten minutes he saw the blonde come into the hallway, followed by Hansen. They stopped at a door. The blonde opened it and the pair went inside. Wilkes slipped out into the hall and positioned himself outside that door.

Harry Lee made his way quickly but silently up the steps. As he reached the second floor he spotted a man in the hall, slightly crouched by one of the doors.

He began to creep down the hall quietly, but another door opened between him and his prey and a girl, startled, shouted, "Hey, whaddaya want?"

The man by the door turned quickly, spotted Harry Lee, and drew his gun. Harry threw himself at the man in a desperate lunge . . .

Willi was grinding her juicy pussy down onto her customer's face, his tongue deep inside of her, his hands clutching her rounded buttocks, when they both heard the shot.

"Oh, shit," she said, because she was so close to an orgasm she could taste it. "Willi ain't gonna get finished tonight."

The man threw her off him and, ignoring the erect organ that protruded from his pants, rushed toward the door, a short-barreled handgun leaping from a shoulder holster into his hand.

Willi, looking down between her legs, saw what looked like part of the man's nose protruding from her pussy, and promptly fainted.

"What are you going to do?" Liz asked the man with the knife.

"I can't have any fun after you're dead," he said. "So I might as well have some before."

He reached down, took a handful of the front of her gown and used the knife to slice it in two. Both ends fell away from her breasts, which tumbled into view. Her nipples were erect but she knew that was from fear, not excitement.

"You got nice ones, all right," he said, licking his lips. "Now, if you lie real still like you're dead, I might not hurt you."

"Bullshit," she said, "you're going to kill me anyway!" She kicked out with her heel and caught him in the balls just as a shot rang out in the hall.

The man reeled back from the blow, but he must have had iron balls, because he neither doubled up nor clutched at his testicles. Instead, he roared out in pain and lunged at Liz as she streaked for the bed, and her gun . . .

Harry Lee's foot struck Wilkes's gun hand just as the man pulled the trigger, and the bullet went up into the ceiling. Off balance, Harry went down onto one knee, and Wilkes moved swiftly, bringing his gun around, catching Harry a glancing blow on the right cheek, stunning him . . .

Inspector Granger — in disguise and with his cock still exposed — rushed out of Willi's room and looked both ways in the hall. Way at the other end he saw Harry Lee, down on one knee with his back to him, while another man stood over him, preparing to blow his head off.

"Hold it!" Granger shouted, extending his own gun and hoping he could get a shot off in time to save Harry's life . . .

Liz tumbled onto the bed, grabbed for the pillow with her right hand and came away with it. The pillow, that is, and just the pillow. The force of her leap took her off the other side of the bed. She had only the pillow to defend herself with, as Hansen advanced on her with his knife . . .

Wilkes risked a glance down the hall at the man with the gun and decided that he was too far away to be an immediate threat. He turned his attention to the man at his feet — but it was the wrong decision.

Granger's shot took him high in the chest, punching every ounce of air out of his lungs. Totally winded, Wilkes staggered back. He panicked, dropped his gun and put both hands up to his throat. Another bullet drove right through his fingers, severing several of them, and took out his throat completely.

As the knife came slashing down at her, Liz held the pillow up as a shield. The blade sliced right through it — only the fact that the pillow was filled with feathers saved her life.

As feathers filled the air, Hansen, his mouth open in a snarl, inhaled several, and began to gag and choke. Seizing her chance, Liz leaped back on the bed, and this time her desperate grab came up with the gun. She braced her back against the headboard and held the gun out in front of her. Red-faced and gasping, Hansen found himself staring down the barrel of Angel Eyes' gun.

Granger hurried down the hall and hauled Harry Lee to his feet.

"Are you all right?" he demanded.

Harry was bleeding freely from a gash on his cheek, but his eyes seemed clear now and he stared at Granger and demanded, "Who the hell are you?"

"Which is Liz's room?" Granger demanded.

As if he suddenly remembered that Liz was alone with Hansen, Harry yelled, "This one!" and together both men began to break down the locked door . . .

The tableau that greeted them was a strange one. Liz, her breasts bare and her gown in tatters, sat back flat against the headboard, her gun held straight out in front of her.

Hansen was staring at her, his wicked blade in his hand and a flurry of white feathers floating in the air around him.

"It's all over, Hansen," Granger said, pointing his own gun at the man.

Hansen looked over at the two men who had just broken into the room, then looked back at Liz.

"Don't be a fool, Hansen," Liz said. "If you make a move you're a dead man."

"I'm a dead man, anyway," Hansen said. "I killed Drake, the Chinese whore, and that dumb cop. I ain't gonna walk away from three killings." He held the knife loosely in his hand as he spoke. Harry wondered idly if the thing was balanced for throwing.

"Well, before you commit suicide," Liz said, "how about telling us who you're working for?"

"Me? I worked for Wilkes, really, but he got his orders — and money — from his boss."

"And who was that?" Granger asked.

"I'll tell you what," Hansen said with a crafty look on his face. "I'll give you a name and you can figure out which one it is."

"A name?" Granger asked.

Hansen grinned and said, "Simonson."

With that he drew his hand back to throw the knife at Liz.

Her gun and Granger's went off at the same time, both slugs slamming into Hansen's big body and throwing him against the wall. His huge weapon, a source of fear for a good many years on the Barbary Coast, fell from his lifeless fingers and quiveringly embedded itself in the wooden floor.

"Guess it was balanced for throwing," Harry Lee said.

Liz got off the bed and moved toward the body. Harry and Granger joined her.

"You're hanging out," Granger said.

She looked at him and was about to ask him who he was when she recognized him as the man who had gone upstairs with Willi.

"You're hanging out, too, Inspector."

He stared at her and said, "How did you know it was me?"

"I don't know what you were doing," Liz said, pulling the remains of her gown over her breasts, "but your phony nose has melted."

CHAPTER THIRTY

THEY FOUND both Edward and Thomas Simonson at the office on Kearny Street.

Granger had removed his makeup and stalked out of the whorehouse. Liz had changed quickly, while Harry went down to talk to Madam Chou. Then she rushed out with Harry Lee in tow. Though Granger was gone, Liz knew where to find him. They all arrived at Kearny Street at the same time, Granger with two of his police officers.

"What about Madam Chou's?" Liz asked.

"I've sent some men there to clean up the mess we left," Granger said. He had cleaned his face and changed his clothes. He looked at Harry, whose cheek was swollen and crusted with dried blood. "You look like shit," he informed Lee.

"Let's get this over with."

"Inspector, you rushed out before I could give you my thoughts — "

"Never mind your thoughts," Granger said. "Why don't

you go home, Miss Archer? You're free and clear.''

"There are several reasons why I can't do that," Liz said stubbornly. "The main one is that I have no home. Shall we go in?''

"After you.''

They found Edward Simonson seated at his desk and Thomas bent over him — a repeat of the pose Liz had first seen them in.

"Inspector Granger," the elder Simonson said, looking up at them.

"I'd like to talk to you, Mr. Simonson.''

"I have no problem with that," Simonson said, "but do you need a mob to do it? And what happened to that man's face?''

"Never mind that, Mr. Simonson," Granger said. "I think you had better come with us.''

"Where? And for what?''

"We have a confession from your man, Hansen, that you hired him and Wilkes — ''

"Wilkes?" Simonson said, frowning. "What the devil has Wilkes got to do with this?''

"You know the man?''

"I know Wilkes," Simonson said. "He was the foreman in one of my warehouses until I fired him a few weeks ago for stealing. The other man I never heard of. What was his name? Hansen?''

"They called him Swede Hansen along the Barbary Coast," Granger explained. "Not your usual class of employee.''

"I don't know what you're talking about, Inspector," Edward Simonson said. "I fired Wilkes and I've never heard of Hansen.''

"He's right," Liz said.

"What?" Granger asked.

"He never heard of Hansen," Liz said. "But Thomas has, haven't you, Thomas?"

"Me? I never heard of the man," Thomas said.

"Sure you did. Wilkes worked for you, so you knew that he had brought in Hansen to do the killing."

"What makes you think I had anything to do with it?"

"The old man's the one with the power," Granger argued.

"Old man?" Edward Simonson said, bristling.

"But the young man wants the power," Liz said. "And what motive would Edward Simonson have had for killing Vincent Drake?"

"Yes," Edward Simonson said. "What motive?"

"To get at Victor Drake."

"If I want to get at Victor Drake I'll do it through my business contacts, not by murder."

"Why would Thomas kill the Drake boy?" Granger asked.

"Why don't you ask him?"

Granger looked at Thomas Simonson as if waiting for an answer.

"If you're waiting for me, Inspector," Thomas said, smoothly, "I have nothing to say."

"Harry? Tell the inspector what Madam Chou told you."

Granger looked at Harry Lee then, his face betraying both confusion and impatience.

"Madam Chou needed money to keep up her payments to the tong," Harry explained. "She got it from him."

"From Thomas Simonson?" Granger asked.

"From you?" Edward Simonson said, looking up at his nephew. "You invested money in a house of debauchery?"

"Invested, hell," Liz said. "He bought it. He and his partner."

"Partner?" Edward Simonson said.

"Madam Chou said his partner was an ugly woman."

"Gabrielle," Edward Simonson said, and it was probably the first time in his life he'd ever admitted out loud that his daughter was ugly. "I'm afraid I don't understand any of this."

"You wouldn't," Thomas said, sneering at his uncle. "You with your high-and-mighty, holier-than-thou attitudes. Gabrielle and I are sick of them. We wanted something better for ourselves."

"You . . . and Gabrielle?"

"It was her idea, actually, but it was a good one."

"You think so, huh?" Harry Lee said. "In a matter of weeks the tongs would have chewed you up and spit you out."

"Rabble," Tom Simonson said, and Harry Lee made a disgusted sound with his mouth.

"But why kill Drake?" Granger said. "And the girl, and Dunn?"

"Drake found out that Gabrielle and I owned Madam Chou's," Thomas Simonson said. "He was going to tell you, Uncle dear. It doesn't take much imagination to guess how you would have reacted."

"I would have thrown you out."

"Me, but not Gabrielle," the younger Simonson said. "She's your daughter. I'm only the son of the woman who shamed your brother."

"I never held that against you," the old man said.

"Like hell," Thomas retorted. "The girl was killed by accident, the policeman because he was in Hansen's way when he went for Liz."

"And what's left to be done?" Edward Simonson asked. "Now you'll both go on trial for murder."

"And your good name will be muddied," Thomas said. "You know, it might almost be worth it . . ." He paused, grinned briefly, then said: "But it's not going to happen."

He flicked his wrist, and suddenly there was a gun in his hand, a two-shot derringer much like the one Liz had been wearing on her thigh. He pressed the barrel against the back of his uncle's head.

"I'm walking out of here, Inspector."

"You going to stop for Gabrielle?" Liz asked.

"Gabrielle," Thomas said, making it sound like a dirty word. "After you, Liz, I could never go back to her. I'll just take what money Uncle Edward has in his safe here and leave San Francisco. You'll never hear from me again, Inspector."

"I'm afraid I can't let you do that, Simonson."

"Why not?" Thomas asked. "It's no skin off your nose. I killed a whore and a useless piece of shit."

"And a policeman," Granger added. "The other two I might overlook, but not the policeman."

"And I won't overlook the girl," Harry Lee said.

Liz looked at Harry, but he was staring at Tom Simonson.

"That derringer only holds two shots, Simonson," Granger said. "It's not gonna get you far."

"The first one will kill the old man." Thomas prodded his uncle's head with the barrel.

"You won't get a chance to fire the second one," Liz warned.

Tom Simonson turned the situation over in his mind, then said, "All right. But I want to make a deal."

"What deal?" Granger asked.

"I don't want to see him buy Gabrielle free," said

Thomas, prodding his uncle's head again. "If I go, she goes too."

"If she's as guilty as you are," Granger said, "she'll certainly go too."

"As guilty as me?" Thomas said, laughing and flipping the derringer to Granger. "She's as guilty as the Devil himself."

CHAPTER THIRTY-ONE

ON HER LAST NIGHT in San Francisco Liz ended up where she'd known all along she would.

In bed with Dan Granger.

Granger did not have the perfect body that Tom Simonson had, but he was certainly more experienced, and in fact was quite well built. Liz Archer was not disappointed.

"You're an incredible woman," he said to her, after they had made love for the second time in an hour, "in more ways than one."

"What ways?"

"You're soft, beautiful and just about the stubbornest woman I've ever known. You knew I was dangling you as bait, but you kept on going."

"And you knew about Hansen all along," she shot back. "Both you and Harry Lee."

"No. We both thought it *might* be Hansen, because of

that blade, but I didn't know who Hansen was working for. For that I needed you.''

"And what was Harry Lee working for?''

"He knew Ling, the girl who was killed. He wanted revenge for her.''

"Was he in love with her?''

"Harry loves his sister, and that's all,'' Granger said. "But that girl was one of his people, one of his friends. He couldn't let her murder go unpunished.''

"Everybody had a stake in this, then,'' Liz said. "Harry Lee's was revenge, Carla's was that she loves you.''

"She liked you — ''

"But she helped me escape for you, Dan. She loves you, and you know it.''

"I know it,'' he said, and didn't try to explain anything to her. She didn't pry, because that would be between him and Carla, after Liz was gone.

"Why'd you take a leave of absence and get all made up the way you did?''

"Steelman wanted to haul you in, Liz,'' Granger said, making circles around one of her nipples with his fore-finger. "I wanted you out there where I could keep an eye on you.''

"Keep me safe, you mean?'' she asked. "Is that what you were doing in Willi's room?''

"I got . . . distracted,'' he said. "I'm only human.''

"Well, I'm impressed.''

"Why?''

"Willi said it was four nights before she finally got you to touch her.''

"She was almost as stubborn as you.''

"It wasn't that,'' Liz said. "You presented a challenge

to her. If you'd bedded her the first night, she wouldn't have bothered you after that.''

''Oh,'' he said, grinning and cupping Liz's breast. ''It was no bother.''

''And you scared her to death when you lost your nose.''

GREAT BOOKS

E-BOOKS

AUDIOBOOKS

& MORE

Visit us today

www.speakingvolumes.us

www.ingramcontent.com/pod-product-compliance
Lightning Source LLC
Chambersburg PA
CBHW022152260626
47155CB00017B/1839